CAESAR'S ANTLERS

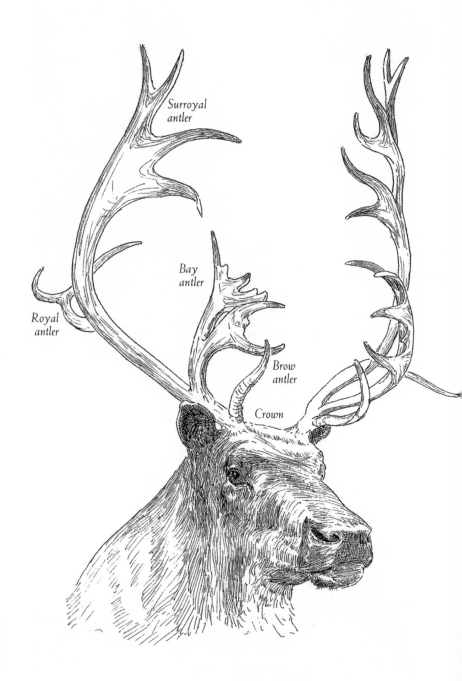

Surroyal
antler

Bay
antler

Royal
antler

Brow
antler

Crown

Hansen

CAESAR'S ANTLERS

With drawings by the author

Farrar, Straus and Giroux
New York

Library of Congress Cataloging-in-Publication Data

Hansen, Brooks, 1965–
    Caesar's antlers / Brooks Hansen ; with drawings by the author. —
1st ed.
        p.   cm.
    Summary: Bette, a mother sparrow separated by accident from her
mate, takes her chicks on a long search when a faithful reindeer
permits her to make a nest in his antlers.
    ISBN 0-374-31024-6
    [1. Reindeer—Fiction.   2. Sparrows—Fiction.   3. Lost and found
possessions—Fiction.   4. Antlers—Fiction.]   I. Title.
PZ7.H19823Cae   1997
[Fic]—dc21   96-53148

PART I

The Brows

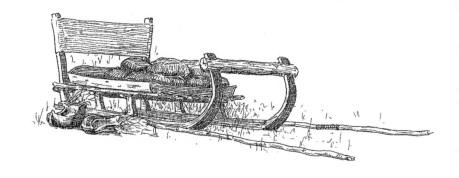

One

The thought first came to Caesar, the same as it did to every member of the herd, borne on a single breeze. He had been grazing on a drift of heather when a northern wind carried it across the pasture to him, the scent of summer's death. The sun was still high and hot, but Caesar knew—he could smell: the air, the color, the sky would soon be changing. The time had come to leave again.

As soon as he finished his meal, he started for the meeting place, at the tundra basin. He met his two younger cousins at the forest's edge, and they climbed the first ridge together. At a fallen spruce, they came upon another band of five reindeer, also from the herd. Caesar welcomed them to his team, and they walked the rest of the way together in silence.

The basin rested at the far end of the tundra beyond the hills—a giant bowl set in the land, itself as large as a meadow but sunk in the ground as if the earth in just that part had lost its breath. Caesar led his company a full day across the flatland, but when they finally came to the basin, he let the others start down the ridge ahead of him. He wanted to survey the gathering from above.

The men were there already, sitting in camps around the ridge. As usual, they'd left the deer to themselves for most of the summer, but now they returned to accompany the herd on its inland trek, from the high hills to the low pastures.

Caesar looked for the brothers, Ole and Gaino. Their sister was on the far side with the children, and Gaino's eldest son, Mikkel, was coming down the slope now with his little boy up on his shoulder, but Caesar didn't see the brothers. They must still be on their way, he thought, and so descended to the basin floor to wait among the deer.

Less than half the herd was there—two hundred head. The rest would arrive by nightfall, but already

4

the men were coming down to sort among them. This was the men's task today, to choose which deer they should name, which they should spay, which they should lead away, never to be seen again. And the deer understood, even the calves. They shifted anxiously at the men's approach, shuffling back and forth with wide eyes and turning heads.

Not Caesar, though. Years ago, on a day like this when Caesar was just a pricket, Ole and Gaino had come down and chosen him, and given him his name. Ever since, Caesar had helped them, led their treks, pulled their sleds, let the children ride on his back. In return he was given food, and allowed to enjoy the warmth of their fires, and their company.

Caesar's cousin Karin was another. Today she was standing at the foot of the ridge, calm outside the larger group.

Caesar greeted her. "Tomorrow?"

"Tomorrow," she replied.

"Is Berit here?"

Karin pulled sleds for Berit's clan; Berit's children had all been raised on Karin's milk.

She nodded across the way. Berit was standing up on the ridge, assessing the herd with her hands on her hips.

"What about Ole and Gaino?" Karin asked.

Caesar shook his head. "Not yet."

They turned back to the deer. The men were roving among them in pairs now, whistling, clicking their tongues, twirling ropes above their heads and landing them on antlers.

Caesar and Karin watched in silence, and slowly a small group of other deer began to gather around them—at first just those who also helped the men. Then others came over one by one, young deer who hadn't names, but who hoped that just by being near, by imitating those who did, they might enjoy the same treatment, might survive this day and start the trek tomorrow.

"Tomorrow?" they greeted one another.

Tomorrow, they nodded in return.

"You don't think it's too early?" one asked Caesar.

Caesar shook his head as a calf nearby was roped and thrown to the ground. The group shuffled to the side.

"Are Ole and Gaino here?" asked another, a gelding.

Caesar shook his head. "Not yet."

He gave a look about the ridge again. There were still deer descending from the tundra, trickling down the shallowest slopes and slowly filling the basin. The herd was beginning to move as one, turning circles within circles like currents. But there was still no sign of his two friends.

Then Caesar felt something brush his antlers. Karin's eyes flashed to their whites, and there came a stiff yank from the side. He'd been roped.

Stunned, the other reindeer stepped clear of the line. At the far end was Mikkel and his little boy, just barely holding on with his hands above his father's head.

"It's all right." Caesar looked up at Karin, his neck still twisted down by the taut line. "It's only Mikkel." There came another hard tug. "Tomorrow."

Tomorrow, she nodded, but her eyes weren't as certain as before.

Mikkel was not angry. As soon as Caesar was clear of the others, the rope relaxed. The boy climbed on Caesar's back and they walked around the outside of the churning herd, up the far ridge to the family camp.

Mikkel's brother was up the slope, honing the runners of a sled with a stone. It was Ole and Gaino's sled, Caesar recognized, the one they used in the winters. Their sister was sitting nearby with the girls, around a small fire with blankets on their knees and cups in their hands. The girls got up and greeted Caesar with hugs, but the sister was busy trussing a small pile of deerskin bundles. Caesar couldn't see what she was stuffing inside, but they were all about the same size. They fit in her lap, and she was tying them fast with gutstring.

As soon as she was done, Mikkel came over and took the bundles to the sled. He and his brother packed them tight along the base, binding them down with more long threads of gut, but they left the back seat open, as if to keep it clear for one small passenger.

Mikkel called Caesar over and slid the harness down onto his neck. Caesar took a step to feel the weight—not too heavy, but he wasn't used to pulling sleds before the snow.

Mikkel went to say goodbye to the family. His sister gave him one last bundle, much smaller than the rest, which he tucked in with the others. Then he and Caesar started up the ridge together.

They paused briefly at the top. The whole herd looked to be there now, drifting back and forth in a golden cloud of dust. The low light of the sun slanted in and caught the velvet of their thousand antlers. Their hooves pounded. Their ankles slapped. The men whistled and clicked and hooted, and the reindeer murmured. Tonight they would spend here in the basin, and tomorrow at dawn they'd leave. But still Caesar did not see Ole and Gaino.

Whth-whth! He felt the snap of Mikkel's whip, and Caesar started.

Caesar traveled the next two days with Mikkel over the high, lonely terrain. Mikkel drove like his father and his uncle, helping whenever the runners of the sled would catch or snag, and walking beside Caesar on the slopes, either up or down. He ate from a satchel he kept around his waist—dried strips of meat, nuts and berries—but he never once touched the bundles on the sled.

They struck a different trail than the herd would follow in the morning. They met the river farther up toward the hills and had to wait for the ferry at dawn to cross. A second day's journey brought them to a forest at the foothills of the great blue ridge. Mikkel led more slowly now, pausing often to touch leaves and check the sky. They passed above a wide blue lake and farther up the surrounding fells until finally, just as the light began to fade, they came upon an open glade.

There was a single tree at the center—black, dead, split down the middle of its trunk. Mikkel led Caesar to a bank of jutting rocks on the far side. There was a small grotto at the base, guarded by a collar of reindeer antlers, all hooked together.

Mikkel knelt down in front of them and waited until the shadow of the dead tree fell across his back.

Then he climbed over the ring of antlers and into the hollow. Caesar could hear a stone slide to the side, and when Mikkel emerged again, he had another bundle in his arms.

This one was slightly larger than the others on the sled, and wrapped in bearskin. Mikkel carried it over the ring of antlers and, with the same care as he might handle an infant child, laid it down on the back seat of the sled. Like all the rest, he tied it with gutstring, then before the sun could see what he had done, he led Caesar back across the glade, past the blackened tree, and down the same path as they'd come.

With the light still fading, they descended to a small ledge above the smooth blue lake. A white mist clung to the heads of the surrounding hills. Mikkel nodded toward the distance, and spoke to Caesar without words. He placed his hand on Caesar's head, and then on his own chest. He set his palms together, flat, then parted them: Mikkel was leaving Caesar here.

He reached inside his coat, and took out a deerskin mitten. He held it up to Caesar's nose—it was Gaino's mitten. Mikkel tucked it in with all the other bundles on the sled, and pointed out across the lake again: Gaino was somewhere on the other side. And Ole, too. Something must have happened. Something was not right.

Mikkel said no more. He dropped a handful of

mushrooms at Caesar's feet, gave him one last chuck on the neck, then started down the path alone.

Caesar did not follow. He listened to Mikkel's feet tramping down the trail, fainter and fainter until all was silent again, and there was only Caesar and the sled, and the lake and the moon.

PART II

The Crown

Two

Piorello and Bette first met on the outstretched hand of a girl who was wearing white flowers in her hair. It was a late summer day, and a brief shower had just swept through the forest when she appeared, as usual, at the bend of the narrow path that looped through the lakeside wood.

For most of the summer the girl had been coming round at this same time with seeds, so when she arrived this day—her golden-brown hair wreathed in white flowers—all the sparrows that lived in that part of the forest alerted one another. They gathered at the tan-

15

gle of junipers that divided the path, and there the young girl stopped. She took a handful of seeds from a small brown bag, and set them in a pile on her palm.

No sooner had she extended her arm than the birds flew down. They came one by one from their various perches, landing on her hand, taking their seeds, and then returning to crack the shells and eat, and wait their turn again.

Piorello and Bette both came late to the feeding, and had chosen opposite sides of the juniper in which to wait, so they did not even see one another at first. Their attention was set too fast on the Seed Girl's hand. When they saw it was free again and that no other birds were coming, the two of them jumped from their separate perches. At the very same moment they swept down toward the girl and landed at once—much to their surprise—right across from each other on her palm.

Neither of the sparrows knew what to do. Their eyes glanced. Bette took her seed, Piorello took his, then both turned and flew back to the spiny perches, as if nothing so odd or extraordinary had occurred, though each knew something had.

The two birds were not unfamiliar with one another, after all. Both were born the summer before, and as members of the same flock, they frequented many of the same trees and bushes. Bette knew Piorello by the brown crescent on the nape of his neck and by his call—a short twist in his throat. But most of all she knew him by his talents in the air. Of all the sparrows in the flock, Piorello was by far the most daring. He cut the swiftest and most pleasing arcs through the trees, but always landed with perfect poise.

Piorello knew Bette by the quality of her song, which was likewise superior to all others in the flock, especially for one of the females, who tended not to sing as well. Bette was an exception, so much so that she was often mistaken, sight unseen, for a meadowlark.

So it was, as Bette and Piorello flew back to their respective perches that late afternoon at the juniper bush, both were well aware of whom they'd just bumped into. As soon as Piorello landed, he looked across at Bette again. He watched her bend to crack her shell, and when she straightened up and saw that she was being watched—and by whom—she became so flustered, she dropped her seed to the ground.

"Wait—" Piorello called across, seizing the moment. In a blink, he whisked back down to the girl, pecked a second seed from her palm, and then ascended to Bette's side of the juniper, sweeping underneath her perch before landing gently beside her.

Bette was startled at first, but when Piorello cracked the shell, removed the seed, and held it out to her, she did accept.

"Bette," he chirped.

"Piorello," she sang.

Piorello. Her voice sounded the name so sweetly, the sparrow could hardly contain himself. He jumped to the branch above her head. "Have you been to the willow?" he asked.

"Where the geese like to nap?"

Piorello nodded.

"But isn't it the cat's?"

He nodded again. "It was, but she hasn't claws anymore. She can't climb." Piorello darted across the path to the branch of a short birch. "Come on!"

Bette followed him. He led her up the path and around the bend until they could see the blue lake through the trees. Another turn and they came to it— a hunchback willow, leaning out over the water and casting down such long and heavy braids, their ends brushed the drifting surface.

"This way." Piorello led her round the side to a small parting in the braids. A stone bath stood underneath, with a small statue in the middle of a woman in a hood, her arms extended low on each side.

"I've been here." Bette stood on the statue's head

and looked in beneath the gray-green shroud. "When I was younger, with my brothers."

Piorello nodded. "But everyone thinks the cat's still here. See?" He flew over the bent trunk and around several limbs before finally coming to rest on the forked branch above the bath. "There's no one. Or no one except the geese, but they only come when it's too hot."

"I see." Bette hopped up next to him. "Thank you for showing me."

Piorello's breast rose up. "Wait here!" He jumped back down to the stone bath and looked up at her. "Don't move." He turned and darted up the path again, out of sight.

Bette stayed on her perch. The bells chimed in the distance. The trees shifted in the afternoon breezes, and she could hear the sparrows summoning one another, but they sounded so far away.

"Piorello?" she called. She waited, but there was no answer. "Piorello?" She listened again, but all she could hear were baying geese, far off. She wondered where he could have gone, and was about to leave her perch to go and look when suddenly—*thrush!*—he came bursting through the lakeside willow braids.

"Here!" he called.

"Piorello, you'll hurt yourself!"

"I won't. Don't worry." He looked at her brightly. "Again." He darted to the stone bath and disappeared up the path, for a second time leaving Bette alone on her limb.

This time, she took the moment to look around. So peaceful. The sky was white where it glanced in through the braids. She watched them stroke the water. Such seclusion, she thought. Such shelter and quiet.

"Piorello?" she called. "Are you there?"

Thrush! He came bursting through the braids again, but this time as he landed beside her, she saw he had a pine needle in his beak.

Bette was taken aback. "But I've never made a nest."

Piorello laid the needle down before her. "Neither have I, but we could try." He jumped up to one of the longer limbs. "What about here?"

Bette considered. She'd never known any of the other sparrows to make their nest in a willow, but as she looked round, she wasn't sure why, or why not, especially now that the cat was gone.

"What do you say?" asked Piorello.

"All right. But not there. It's too high."

Piorello hopped to a lower branch and presented it. "Here?"

No, Bette shook her head again. "Too exposed."

The next spot Piorello tried was apparently too

dark, and the one after that too cold. In fact, it wasn't till he returned to the very branch where she was waiting—the forked one—that Bette, with a wag of her tail feathers, finally consented.

"Good," he said, and flew straight off to gather what they'd need before Bette could change her mind.

She didn't. They spent the afternoon building their nest of pine needles and dried twigs and bristles from the forest floor. Piorello brought them up to Bette in bunches, which she took and twisted around a small nub near where the branches forked. She wove them together into a cup, which she lined with moss that Piorello brought, and dog hairs and raven feathers.

The light outside was just beginning to fade when finally Bette refused Piorello's last offering—a tuft of goose down. She stepped back from their work. "That should do, I suppose."

"Do?" Piorello let the tuft drop. "More than do." He jumped inside. "It's very sturdy." He huddled down. "And warm. Why, I should think that any bird would consider himself lucky to call such a nest home."

"And such a tree."

The forest outside murmured, then crackled. They looked up through the ribbons of green. It was beginning to rain.

"It's all right," Piorello said. "Nothing much comes through." He climbed out of the nest to perch beside

21

her, and she noticed a small thistle stuck to his nape. She bent to pluck it.

"Thank you." He bowed his head, and so their evening was set. While the sky and the whole world out beyond the willow fell a darker and darker shade of blue, Bette and Piorello perched beside each other, grooming. They listened to the rain trickling down the braids. They watched the water in the stone bath rise, and when the darkness had fallen completely, they climbed inside their nest and spent their first night together, warm and safe and dry.

In the coming days, Bette and Piorello barely left each other's sight. When the sun was out, they flew some with the flock. They met the others at the juniper bush when the girl came out with her seeds, but they told no one of their private place, where they returned each night. The only ones who ever saw them at the willow were the greylag geese who sometimes used the tree for shade, but even they, when they saw the sparrows return, would float off quietly to leave the young birds be.

"And I am yours," Bette would sing.

"Yours forever," answered Piorello. He'd fly around the branches while she watched. "The two of us, Bette—we are one now."

"Yes, we are one, the two of us."

"One forever—Bette and I."

"And I and Piorello," she'd reply.

It wasn't long before such devotion yielded more, and Bette laid three pale green eggs at the bottom of their nest.

Neither she nor Piorello went flying with the other sparrows after that. They had to make sure to keep the eggs as safe and warm as possible. Bette sat through the night, and they took turns sitting in the mornings and afternoons.

The geese who lolled beneath the willow could not help but note. "Such a sunny day," they'd call up. "I'd expect to see you out among the birches, Piorello. Does this mean good news?"

"Very good news, yes," he'd answer, but he said no more until ten days passed, and a tiny beak chipped through the first of the little green shells. He and Bette watched together as an infant chick wriggled out. "A son!" cried Piorello. "A son!"

"Congratulations," said a goose, leaning underneath the shroud. "And what's his name?"

"Pavel," Bette replied.

Just then there came a little tapping sound, as a tiny beak chipped through the second shell, and a second chick sprung free. "A daughter!" proclaimed the father.

23

"Whose name shall be Rhone," Bette said.

The parents turned their eyes to the third of the eggs in the nest, but it did not move. While the geese drifted below expectantly, Bette and Piorello looked at the third shell and waited, but it remained round and still. "You go," Bette said to Piorello. "I'll wait here, but Pavel and Rhone need food."

Piorello agreed, and flew off quick. He went to find some grass seed, enough for three nestlings, but when he returned to the willow, he saw the geese were gone, and the third egg was down on the ground, pushed from the nest.

He looked up. Bette was leaning out, shaking her head sadly. "I'm sorry," she said.

Piorello flew the seeds up and set them in the nest. "It's all right," he said. "You'll see. Pavel and Rhone will keep us busy enough. And we'll be one, like you and I. Except now there's four of us. Pavel and Rhone and Bette and I. Sing, Bette."

"Yes," she answered gamely. "You and I." She looked at her two newborn. "And Pavel, and his sister, Rhone."

"But you rest now, Bette, and I'll find us both something to eat."

She gave a quiet nod and Piorello left.

He followed the walk this time, all the way to the tall green lawn with the great white house that faced the lake. There was a feeder there, hanging from the limb of a beech tree—it was gabled and made of birch bark, and it was always filled with Bette's favorite millet.

Piorello was taking grains for her when he heard a strange, faint chiming sound coming from the house. He looked its way and was stopped by an image in the corner window: a flower, like the ones the Seed Girl had been wearing in her hair the day that he and Bette had met. It was standing there, up straight, its petals gleaming white in a shaft of slanting light.

I shall take it back to Bette, he thought. I shall crown our nest with that white flower. He jumped from the peg of the feeder and made his way directly. He whisked above the tall green grass and was headed directly for the blossom. He was going to pluck it from its place and take it back to Bette, but just as he opened his beak to grab hold of the stem, the sky turned suddenly flat, and the world fell black. The last he saw was his own image flashing toward him, and the last he heard was the shattering of glass.

Three

Elsbeth had been playing the piano in the parlor when she heard the window in the library break. It was the last day of her summer holiday, and she and her Uncle Per, who played the violin, had come down for one final round of duets together.

They both stopped straight when they heard the glass crunch. Uncle Per lifted his bow and cocked his head. "Tibel?"

Elsbeth ran to see, through the front hall, skidding in her socks right up to the open threshold of the library.

So blue. Even on bright days such as this—blue and cool, untouched by the warmth of a fire, or even a lamp. The library was Tibel's room now, the house elf. It had been her grandfather's favorite before he died, home to all his books and trophies and the largest hearth in the home, but ever since his death, the library had more or less been taken over by Tibel, and the household had learned to respect this. Not even Marta the cat would go in now. The only one who ever did was the housekeeper, Miss Gulbrandsen, and that was only to dust or change the flowers.

"Tibel?" Elsbeth leaned in. "Are you there?"

Uncle Per came up behind her. "Tsk." He nodded across to the corner. There was a lily standing in the bay window. One of the panes was broken, and down on the ledge was the body of a sparrow.

"Tibel?" Elsbeth tried again. "I'm coming in."

She waited, but there was no answer.

"I'll be in the kitchen," whispered Uncle Per. He gave her a tap with his bow and left.

Elsbeth took a deep breath and entered, just a step at first. Even there she could feel—the air was different. Breathless. She gave a look around. She'd never actually seen Tibel herself, but her grandmother and Miss Gulbrandsen had pointed out his telltale signs—a spill on the floor, a tilted painting, a fallen book.

She didn't notice any. All the shelves were in order,

27

the stone hearth yawned black and hollow, and over her shoulder her grandfather's trophies hovered, as always, in perpetual conference: there was the bust of the reindeer, hanging; the great brown bear, rearing up and snarling with his paws extended; and, beside it, the stuffed snowy owl, perched on his pedestal, his scowling eyes trained on whoever chose to enter. Elsbeth could feel them on the back of her neck as she hurried across to the window.

She was almost there when suddenly her brother appeared on the far side, his face bright with excitement.

"Flew right smack into it!" He looked up at her. "And you shouldn't be in there."

"We're allowed." She knelt on the seat cushions, careful to avoid the broken glass. "And you're supposed to be putting away the croquet set."

Miles lifted his lip and turned his attention back to the bird. "See," he instructed, "that would never have happened to a bat." He touched the brown crescent on the sparrow's nape. "We should probably bury it, though."

"How do you know it's even dead?"

Miles opened the sparrow's wing and let it dangle. "Looks dead."

"Doesn't mean it is." She reached to fold the wing closed, but Miles pulled away.

"Besides, you want it to go to heaven, don't you?" He glared at her with wide, daring eyes, then turned from the window, bird in hand, and headed in the direction of the toolshed beneath the porch.

Elsbeth bolted from the sill, back to the front hall. She didn't even bother to put on her shoes. She scuttled down the porch steps, but by the time she came around to the shed door, Miles was already selecting a trowel from the wall hooks.

"Where's the bird?" she asked.

"In the glove." He showed her. He'd taken one of his grandmother's old gardening gloves and tucked the bird inside.

"What for?"

"So the dog won't smell it and dig it up." He nodded for her to clear the door, and started out.

The two of them crossed the lawn together, past all the twisted wickets and tilted posts of the croquet set.

"Where are you going to do it?"

"Don't know." He stopped and looked back at the house shiftily. "I'd rather Miss *Gulburp*sen didn't see."

"Down here, then." Elsbeth pointed to the wood's edge, to the bird-walk. "I know where."

· · ·

"Piorello?" called Bette. "Piorello?" She'd suspected he was only playing one of his tricks, and that at any moment he'd come bursting through the willow braids. He was taking an unusually long time, though, and the chicks were yearning with their beaks, so she began to wonder. "Piorello?"

"Bette?" came an answer, but it was her cousin's voice, Emil's. He appeared on the bath below and looked up. "Bette, what are you doing here?"

"You haven't seen Piorello, have you?"

"No." He jumped to her branch and peered inside the nest. "Are these yours?"

"Ours," replied Bette.

"Piorello?"

She nodded. "But he went off to look for seed, and hasn't returned."

"Well, he's going to miss out." Emil turned. "Look who's coming."

Down at the bend in the path, the girl appeared. She was with the boy from the house, and there was a small flurry of birds, flitting above them eagerly.

It didn't appear she had any seeds with her, though. She walked with an oddly solemn air all the way to the foot of the willow, stopped, and pointed at the ground next to the bath. The boy knelt down. He had a blunt blade with him, which he began stabbing at the dirt. The girl knelt, too, and watched. When he'd managed a hole as deep as his wrist, he held out his hand. The girl passed him a small bundle, and he set it down at the bottom of the hole. The boy muttered something in their strange, garbled tongue. The girl repeated the phrase. Then in unison they both touched their foreheads, their chests, and their shoulders, left to right. The boy took up his blade again, but just as he was about to scoop a clump of dirt from the pile beside the hole, there came a loud squawk from up the pathway.

A stout woman appeared at the bend. She stopped when she saw them, set her hands on her hips, and squawked again.

The boy waited until she was done, then replied with a sour shake of his head, but the woman stood firm. She stamped her foot and pointed in the direction of the house.

Finally the boy relented. Just the boy. He pushed himself to his feet and started back up the path, but so slowly that the woman gave him a sound whack in the rear as he passed.

The girl remained kneeling beside the bath, and there was something secretive in her manner now, like a cat. She waited for her brother and the woman to round the bend, then she reached down in the hole and removed the bundle. She peeked inside, then stood up herself, tucked the bundle inside the pocket of her dress, and started up the path as well.

All the birds of the flock looked on, puzzled. Some

left, some followed her a ways, Bette's cousin included. They followed her to the bend, but when they saw how quickly she turned, they dispersed, and once again Bette found herself alone.

"Piorello?" she called. "Piorello?"

. . .

Miles was uprooting the first post of the croquet set when Elsbeth passed him on the lawn. He looked up suspiciously. "Where are you going?"

"To make a cross."

"You didn't leave the bird, did you?"

Elsbeth showed him the glove and stuck out her tongue.

"All right. Just don't take too long."

She entered the porch shed and closed the door tight behind her. First thing, she removed the sparrow from the glove. Miles was wrong, she knew. "You'll be all right." She stroked his feathers. "You'll see."

On the shelf was a row of brown paper bags, each filled with a different kind of seed or bulb or pod or bean. Elsbeth chose a bulb from the one marked "lily"—it was about the size of a sparrow—and slipped it inside the glove. Then she took one of her grandmother's tomato stakes, split it across her knee, and tied the halves together in the shape of a cross. It wasn't very sturdy, but she didn't want to take too long and rouse suspicion, so as soon as she got the sticks to hold, she gently tucked the bird back inside the pocket of her dress, took up the cross and the glove—with the bulb inside—and left.

Miles was waiting for her on the lawn, now clear of all the wickets, posts, and mallets. He sneered when he saw the cross. "Well, that'll last about two days."

"It's all she had."

"You've got the bird?"

Elsbeth patted her dress and skipped to his side, and the two of them made their way back to the walk.

.　.　.

"Piorello?" Bette was still calling, for her mate had yet to return from his errand. "Piorello?" The forest remained silent, though, until once again a flurry of sparrows came up the path, flitting and twitting above the girl and the boy.

Again they walked directly to the foot of the willow and resumed their places beside the bath. This time, the girl handed the boy a pair of crossed sticks, which he took by the long end and jammed deep inside the hole. The girl set the bundle down beside it gingerly, then the two of them began shoveling the dirt back in, packing it down until the ground was level and the stake stood straight.

Once again they murmured something, then brushed their foreheads and shoulders in unison. The boy stood and wiped his knees, the girl did the same, and they started up the path again, in the same solemn air as they'd come.

As before, the birds followed a ways before dispersing, disappointed. As before, Bette remained in her nest with Pavel and Rhone, now more worried than ever.

"Piorello?" she called. "Piorello?"

.   .   .

Elsbeth and her brother parted ways at the lawn. Miles headed off to the pier for one last round of fishing, and Elsbeth returned to the house, secretly cradling the bird in her pocket.

She went straight upstairs, and was headed up the second flight when she heard her grandmother's voice. "There was an accident?"

Elsbeth descended to her door. Gramma was sitting at her window, looking out at the lake.

"Miles dropped a glass."

Gramma nodded, but kept her eye on the water. "And when will I see you and your brother next?"

"Father says next summer perhaps. He said he might be able to come over from London."

Gramma smiled vaguely, unassured. She pointed to her bedside table. "Could you check the drawer for me?"

Elsbeth went and opened it.

"Is there a box inside?"

There was—a flat silver box. Elsbeth showed her.

"I thought I saw Tibel put something in there. It's for you, I think." She tapped her lap. "Let's see."

Elsbeth went and sat at her grandmother's feet. Carefully she lifted off the cover. Inside, resting on a bed of cotton, was a silver chain and locket with a picture of the Virgin Mary.

Gramma smiled. "Well, where do you suppose he found that? I think that's the one your mother took away to school when she was your age."

Elsbeth turned it over. There were her mother's initials on the back. "Thank you," she said softly.

"Thank Tibel."

"Thank you, Tibel." Elsbeth rested her head on her grandmother's knee. "Maybe you could come over to England. Do you think? For Christmas?"

Gramma smiled and looked out the window. "I'll be here, I suspect."

"You're not even going south to Christiania?"

"I don't think so."

Elsbeth looked down at the lake. Miles was in his boat, perfectly still, fishing. "But doesn't it get awfully dark and cold?"

"It does." Gramma began to stroke Elsbeth's hair. "But it's a different light. Your mother didn't mind when she was a girl. She preferred it." She gave a gentle tug. "But London won't be so bad. London's very nice at Christmas."

"I suppose."

"Are your things all packed?"

Elsbeth nodded absently.

"You should make sure. Mr. Doogan will be back soon."

Elsbeth pulled herself up. "Thank you, Gramma." She kissed her on both cheeks. "Thank you." Then she headed off to her room again, with the bird and her new locket.

There really wasn't much left to do. Most of what she needed for school her father would send from London, and all the rest was nearly packed. She had a steamer trunk and a carpetbag full of clothes, a waterproof wrapper for rugs and cloaks, a square handbag, an umbrella, and a hatbox.

This last was on her bed, and Marta, the calico cat, was curled up on top. Elsbeth pushed her off onto the floor, and removed the lid. There were three dolls inside, two porcelain, one rag, and a stuffed rabbit. She cleared a small space between them and set down her mother's locket.

"Go on now, Marta." She chased the cat out the door and closed it. Then she took the bird from her pocket. She gave his feathers a stroke. "You'll be all right, you'll see." She kissed him on the head and set him down as well, among all the soft frills.

The lid was resting on her pillow. Elsbeth took the scissors from her dresser drawer and punched seven holes through the cardboard top. "You'll see," she said again, sliding the lid down over the box. She covered them all in shadow—the dolls, the locket, and the bird—then sat on her bed to wait for Mr. Doogan.

Four

Bette waited the night in her nest, with Pavel and Rhone under her wing. She called and called for Piorello, but no answer came. In the morning, she summoned her cousins and brothers to bring seeds and grubs for the nestlings, and she asked if they'd help look for her mate. They flew from the lake's edge all the way to the road, but none returned with an encouraging word. No one had seen Pavel and Rhone's father, not even the geese.

A second night fell. The tree seemed darker to Bette now, and more confining. She wished she could go and look for Piorello herself, but with the chicks sleeping under her wing, she knew she had to stay. All she could do was call his name, over and over and over again.

"Piorello? . . . Piorello?"

All through the night she kept up her lament, but heard no answer until the full moon was high and passing over. Then out of nowhere, a snowy owl appeared, standing on the bath beneath her.

"You." He looked up at her with a grave brow. She'd never seen a breast so white. "You call for Piorello."

"Yes," she said, "my mate. Have you seen him?"

The owl shook his head. "He cannot hear you anymore."

Bette's heart clutched at the words.

"He's been taken away," the owl said.

"Away? But where?"

The owl only shook his head again. "Across the water."

Bette looked out at the lake, confused. Across the water? But she'd never even seen the other side. "Is he all right?" she asked. She looked back down, but the owl was gone now—had vanished, as if he'd never been.

A dream, thought Bette—a dream was all. And yet she could feel, she knew, what the owl had said was true. Piorello was somewhere far away.

But where? she wondered. And why? They were to be so happy.

She huddled in her nest the rest of the night, sleepless, wondering what she should do. If she could only go, she would. She'd fly around the lake and look, but she could feel the hearts of her young, murmuring beneath her. They slept the whole night through, fast and sound, but Bette had never felt so alone.

Finally, dawn arrived. The faint light of morning came needling through the leaves and branches, but Bette was still too sad to answer. There seemed no hope without Piorello, but then she heard a sound—a strange *click-clack click-clack*—coming through the wood, closer and closer, then slowing down, then stopping right there at the edge of the willow.

Bette could just barely see him through the braids—a low, sturdy animal, pulling a sled. He had a coarse brown coat, a long muzzle, and gentle black eyes offset by a ring of white fur. But most remarkable of all was the pair of antlers which balanced on top of his head. They rose up from between his ears, three shelves of twisted tines and branches, which brushed and nuzzled the willow braids as he stood there, quietly feeding on the leaves.

"Hello," Bette called. "Down there, with the branches on your head?"

The reindeer's eyes turned up. "Yes?"

"Where are you coming from?"

"My herd." His voice was calm and deep.

"And where are you headed now?"

"The far side of the lake," he said. "A ways." He took another length of willow in his mouth.

Bette watched as his antlers grazed the braids. "Can I ask you a favor?"

The reindeer looked up again.

"I have lost my mate," she said. "He's been taken across the water, and I would like to go and look for him, but I cannot leave my young." She paused. It seemed so much to ask. "I was wondering if you might let us take nest in your antlers. Then I could search for Piorello, and tend to my chicks at the same time."

The reindeer lowered his head to think. He chewed a moment—but only a moment—then he said, "Very well. But I can only take you where the path is clear, where my sled can go."

"That's fine," said Bette. "It's just that I don't think I can wait any longer."

The reindeer gave an understanding nod, then he tilted his head to offer his branches.

She chose the second shelf of his right antler. There were two small tines she could set the nest against. The reindeer lifted his head as high as he could and his antlers just barely reached. He gently hooked the nest. The chicks stirred in their sleep, only barely aware, as the nest settled down into place.

Bette fastened it as quickly as she could. She used some stray twigs to wind around the tines. She worked fast and anxiously, though the reindeer stood without complaint, eating his willow.

"Thank you," she kept saying, "and I promise we won't be a bother."

The reindeer did not seem concerned. He just chewed quietly until the nest was safe and secure.

"There," she said. "I think that should hold."

The reindeer gave a faint nod. "Ready?"

"Yes. And thank you again . . . I don't even know your name."

"Caesar," said the reindeer.

"Caesar," she replied. "Well, I am Bette, and the chicks are Rhone and Pavel."

The reindeer's large black eyes turned up kindly. "Welcome, Bette, and Rhone and Pavel."

With that, he started off. Caesar pulled his sled across the bird-walk and headed through the birches, his hooves and ankles slapping, while the runners of his sled whispered across the first fallen leaves and needles of the season.

PART III

The Bays

Five

Piorello awoke to find the world all dark, except for seven pricks of light above, like seven stars. It was too dim to make out where he was. He felt what seemed like leaves surrounding him. He fluttered his wings—leaves or flowers of some kind, but he couldn't see.

" 'Lo," he called out. "Bette? . . . Bette?"

His eyes were suddenly flooded by light. There was the face of a girl looking down at him—the Seed Girl from the path, speaking to him in her odd, girl tongue.

She reached for him, but Piorello was still too

groggy to resist. She lifted him out into an unfamiliar place—a small room. There was a boy lying asleep across from them. Piorello recognized him as well— the boy who liked to catch fish on the lake—but it was the large peephole in the wall that caught Piorello's attention. It opened to such a peculiar, disturbing view: Of water. Water and sky, and nothing dividing them.

But where am I, thought Piorello. And where is Bette?

"*Shshshshsh,*" the girl stroked his head, which was very sore, come to think of it. The boy stirred in his sleep, and the girl whispered more of her strange, foreign song to him before setting him back down among the leaves and flowers. He could see now, it was a strange sort of nest, with smooth gray sides, and filled inside with all kinds of ruffles and rags, but before he could tell much more, all fell black again. The girl had covered the nest and was now taking him out to a wide-open space. He could hear the booming, whooshing sound of open air and crashing water, and he could feel the ground sway beneath them as if they were perched at the end of a long limb.

For a moment, the cover opened a crack. Piorello saw the sky and flew, just to be free. He darted up to see: they were out upon the most enormous lake. There was no land in sight, just the water and the sky.

Then suddenly, the wind grabbed hold and threw him down on a wood-plank floor with a *whump*.

Instantly the girl was upon him. She held him up to her face and scolded him, then started across the open space. Piorello wasn't sure where for, she held him so tight in her hand, but in a moment the wind fell dead again.

Now she let him see. They were in another small room, but there were no people, just stacks and bundles and gleaming boxes.

The girl set him down inside his smooth gray nest again and spoke another line of gibberish. He didn't know what she could possibly mean to say, but then, with an odd, upbeat nod, she covered the nest halfway, and left.

All was quiet. Piorello could hear the wind whistling outside and the water smashing below. He could feel the room sway, but here inside, all was still and silent. He hopped back out of the nest.

" 'Lo," he called. "Bette? . . . Bette?"

He looked about, but heard no answer. Nothing budged.

"Bette? . . ."

Then, just as suddenly as she'd gone, the girl was back. Piorello jumped up to the highest perch. He didn't want her trying to hold him anymore. But then he saw she'd brought a small dish of water. She set it down for him, and held out a palmful of crumbs.

He was hungry. And thirsty. So, very cautiously, he hopped back down to her. He jumped onto her hand and began to feed, he couldn't help himself. He ate till her palm was bare, and had a drink of water. When he was done, the girl lifted him up to her freckled face and sang her jumbled song. Then she set him down inside the smooth gray nest and left him there, again.

Two days passed. Piorello spent most of the time inside the cold nest, nuzzling behind the rags and ruffles for warmth. He called for Bette every so often, in hopes she might be near, might have awakened in one of these boxes, but the only answer that ever came— and rarely—was the girl, peering down in at him like some giant smiling fool.

Horrible creature! With her long hair dangling about her face, and her voice, so mocking and pretty. He'd have pecked her, he'd have plucked her hair in clumps, except that she always brought food—a not very appetizing selection of bread crumbs, berry seeds, crushed nuts. That was all, and she insisted on watching him. She watched him eat and watched him bathe, and then she'd leave again. Always. She'd set him back inside the cold gray nest and go, and all Piorello could do was sit and wonder.

For that was the worst of it—not the darkness or the confinement, not the rolling tide or the ache in his head. Worst of all was not knowing where he was, or where Bette was. Worst was the sinking feeling that with each passing moment, he was being taken farther and farther away from her, from home, and from his newborn, Pavel and Rhone.

After two days, the girl finally came and took him away from that terrible, lonely room, but outside was no better: a commotion of wind and voices, bumping and shoving. Finally, they boarded a carriage. Piorello could hear the clip-clopping of a horse as they staggered off, but the girl had set him somewhere on top, so it was an awful journey from there, with all the rags and ruffles flip-flopping around him.

They stopped just once. Piorello wasn't sure why at first, but then from the distance he heard some horrendous wheezing monster come chugging up and screech to a halt right next to them. It idled there a moment, searching for prey—Piorello held his breath—then the monster left again just as loud and brutish as it had come.

Only then, when all was safe, did the girl come out and bring Piorello down inside the carriage with her. The horse started off again, and the two of them endured the rest of the journey together, pitching and lurching in the backseat until finally, just as daylight was beginning to fade, they stopped at the top of a small green hill.

Once again there was a bustle of voices and thumps and bumps. This time Piorello's nest was carried up two flights, down a long quiet space, and into a smaller room, where he was set down on a soft bed, flat and still.

.   .   .

It seemed like an awfully small room to Elsbeth. It had a sloped ceiling on one side, a single window, a small fireplace, a bed, a desk, and a dresser. And it seemed even smaller when Mr. Doogan set her bags down on the floor.

"Would you like help unpacking?"

"No, thank you, Mr. Doogan."

He stood at the door. "Anything else then, Miss Elsbeth?"

"No. Thank you, Mr. Doogan."

"I'll see you Christmas, then—not before?"

"No, Mr. Doogan, not before."

A knock sounded at the door. "Hello?" It was Elsbeth's cousin Abigail. "Elsbeth! There you are!" She entered—all freckles and eyeglasses, and orange-blond hair.

"Hello, Abigail. Mr. Doogan, you remember my cousin Abigail."

"Of course, miss."

"Elsbeth, I'm just down the hall. Can you imagine? We're on the same floor. And Emily, too."

"That's nice."

" 'Nice.' Do you hear, Mr. Doogan? I don't think Elsbeth realizes how—" She stopped herself and peered at Mr. Doogan. "Why, Mr. Doogan, what's that you're hiding behind your back?"

He gave a sheepish smile. "Just something from Miss Elsbeth's father." He showed them a flat square box tied with silk ribbon. "He sends his best."

Elsbeth took the box from him, but she didn't open it. She didn't want to.

Mr. Doogan understood. He touched the door knob. "I'll be going, then."

"Yes, Mr. Doogan. Thank you, and thank you for this."

"I'll tell your father." He tipped the brim of his cap. "Miss Abigail."

"Mr. Doogan."

He shut the door behind him, leaving the two girls.

Abigail eyed the box. "Well?" she said, "aren't you going to open it?"

They both sat on the bed. Elsbeth pulled off the ribbon and the lid, and then drew back the soft white wrapping paper.

It was a crimson scarf. "Ooooh," cooed Abigail. "It's as soft as a goose. Feel. And I love the color. Put it on." They both stood up. "It's beautiful."

"Yes."

"Well, you don't seem very excited."

"No, I am."

"I'll take it if you don't want it."

"No, it's fine."

"It's nicer than fine." Abigail bounced back down on the bed again and noticed the hatbox. "And what's this?" She tapped the lid. "Another gift?"

"Careful." Elsbeth started over, but before she could stop her, Abigail had opened the lid. Her eyes danced about the contents, then all of a sudden she let out a shriek.

Out flew the bird, so frightened he nearly bumped his head against the ceiling. He whisked all the way around the molding before finally alighting on the mantel.

Abigail was still squealing, though, and covering her head.

"Shshsh!" Elsbeth crossed to the window and pulled the shutters closed.

"But what was he doing in there?"

"I put him there," Elsbeth whispered harshly. "He's from my grandmother's." She approached the mantel and spoke in a more comforting tone. "There, little bird. Don't be frightened."

Three firm raps sounded on the door. "Ladies?" It was an older woman's voice. "Is there a problem, ladies?"

Elsbeth shot a withering look at her cousin, and went to answer. "No, ma'am." She opened the door just a crack.

"May I?"

Elsbeth stepped back and a beefy woman in a black gown and a white hood entered. "I am Sister Poole," she said. She had a broad chin and a thin line for a mouth. "You must be Elsbeth Bonner."

"Yes, Sister."

The woman looked straight at the bird, who was still perched on the mantel. "And is that what all the screaming was about?"

"It surprised us." Abigail stood, straightening her skirt.

"It flew in the window," said Elsbeth.

Sister Poole glanced dubiously at the shutters.

"I closed them," Elsbeth tried to explain. "I didn't want him to hit the glass."

The sister shook her head impatiently. "And how do you expect him to get out, then?" She crossed to the window, opened the shutters, and threw up the sash. "Come along." She waved to the bird. "Shoo."

The bird stayed perched on the mantel, perplexed, so the sister marched up and took him in hand. Before Elsbeth could think how to stop her, the sister crossed back to the window and tossed the bird out.

"There now." She brushed off her hands. "That wasn't so difficult, was it?"

"No, Sister." The two girls bowed their heads.

. . .

Piorello was at a loss. He found himself aloft in a rag-white sky, above a square courtyard bordered on three sides by red-brick buildings and then, across the way, a small gray chapel. He made for the high ledge of the spire, where a covey of fat pigeons was nestled in the corners, cooing. None seemed to noticed his arrival, though, so Piorello hopped up to the very peak of the spire to get a better view.

It was a whole compound of red-brick buildings, set in the midst of a green and rolling countryside. There was just one road leading up, with a small trail of black carriages still making their way. Down below, the grounds were crowded with girls in skirts and kneesocks and hats with ribbons. They were running from door to door, holding their hats to their heads and screeching at one another, while older gentlemen in black suits struggled behind with heavy bundles.

Here and there the girls clustered in circles, sur-rounding women dressed like the one who'd just ex-pelled him from the room, in gowns with hoods.

Strange place. Strange smell. Piorello didn't like it.

Then all at once the pigeons on the ledge took note of something below. They waddled to the lip and looked down. One of the hooded women was making her way along the path. The pigeons leaned out expectantly as she took a seat on a bench. Then as she slipped her hand inside the pocket of her gown they all flocked down. Before she cast her first hand-ful of seeds she was already surrounded.

Piorello realized he was hungry, too. He flew down after the pigeons and landed in their midst.

Such bedlam he could never have imagined. A frenzy of thrashing gray wings and darting beaks. The pigeons looked at him with cold black eyes—who are you, they seemed to say, and where did you come from? They whisked him aside and shoved him with their tails, and if he managed to get his beak on so much as a crumb, they'd peck at him and steal it straight away. It was hopeless. Soon the hooded woman was out of feed entirely. The pigeons swept the ground clear and returned to their ledges. Piorello hadn't eaten a single grain.

"You'll have to be quicker than that."

Piorello turned to see there was a Saint Bernard slumped contentedly beside the bench, his great sloppy muzzle draped across his paws.

"But they're awfully big, the pigeons."

The Saint Bernard lifted his ear curiously. "You're not from here."

"No," said Piorello. "I'm from a birch forest across the water."

The dog was impressed. "One of the girls bring you?"

"Yes." Piorello sighed. "And I'd like to get back as soon as I can. The problem is"—he looked around at the sky and all the buildings—"I haven't the faintest idea where we are."

The dog gave a look around himself. "Can't help you. Never been past the valley." He tried to nudge a smile from Piorello, but failed.

"Oh, now, don't worry. It's not so bad. Bit rainy, but that helps keep things green. Nice big forest for you, and the company's friendly enough. The sisters always have something in their pockets, and the girls'll treat you well." He nodded over Piorello's head. "Is that yours there?"

Piorello looked back. The Seed Girl was leaning out her window now, scanning the grounds with an expression of great distress. "She's not mine, but yes." He hopped beneath the bench so she wouldn't see.

"She doesn't look so terrible."

"You wouldn't say that if you knew her."

The girl pulled back inside and closed the shutters.

"Maybe." The dog gave a yawn and checked the sky. It looked ready to rain. "I'm just saying—if I were as hungry as you look, and that was the window of the girl who'd brought me, I'd go there."

He stretched, gave a farewell nod, and lumbered off, just as the first drops of rain began to splinter down. The girls all began to squeal and run inside. Two beads plunked Piorello on the head and tail. "Oh, all right." He looked back up at the girl's window. "But just till it passes."

He could see as he flew up, the girl was gone. All was dark behind the shutter slats. But when he landed on the sill, he found two dishes waiting for him: one filled with seeds; the other, a shallow pool of water.

S i x

To find Piorello. This remained Bette's goal, first and last—to seek out sight, or sound, or word of her lost mate. And for this purpose, the antlers of her kind host served well. While Caesar proceeded on his steady click-clacking path around the great lake, Bette was able to tend to Pavel and Rhone, to find them seeds and worms with no fear of leaving them unattended, and also to keep up the search. Everywhere they passed, she called for Piorello, and whenever Caesar would pause to feed on heather or to strip the beards of lichen from the old pine trunks, she would go explore the surrounding wood, to ask if any of the animals nearby might have seen a lone sparrow recently. If she happened upon an otter chewing on a fallen stump, she'd fly down and ask; or a squirrel collecting nuts. Any creature she could find, she would ask, but the answer was always the same. No, they had not seen any such bird. So Bette would return to Caesar's antlers, and Caesar would return to his trail.

She tried not to lose heart, or ever let Pavel and Rhone see her disappointment. She always brought back seeds with her, and worms and grubs. Caesar would hold his head steady while she fed them. Then when they were full and tired, Bette would perch beside the nest. Caesar's gait would rock them gently, and Bette would make a lullaby of Piorello's name, just in case he might be near, and hear them passing.

So it was that Pavel and Rhone grew from chicks to fledglings. On the bay-tine of Caesar's left antler, their eyes first opened. From its height, they first beheld the forest, and at Caesar's unfailing pace they watched it pass, the birches always deep and tall to the left, and the great lake looming through the trees on the right.

Caesar did not falter. At times the sled would catch on a fallen branch or they might come upon a creek, but Caesar did not ever complain or tarry. He would simply lean in and pull the sled through its snag, or walk it up to the shortest, shallowest pass he could find, and continue on.

On their fourth day together, just as the first traces of feathers appeared against the nestlings' down, Caesar stopped beside a small stream to ruminate. As was her custom, Bette took the moment to survey the wood nearby. She flew up the creek to see if there was anyone along the banks, and around the bend she came upon a beaver, spanking the mud of a new dam with his broad flat tail.

"Excuse me." She flew down, little knowing as she spoke that a hungry gyrfalcon was perched on the limb of a nearby birch, eavesdropping.

"Excuse me. I'm sorry to take you from your work, but I wonder if you might have crossed paths with a sparrow named Piorello recently?"

The beaver looked up quickly and shook his head.

"He's brown and tan like me," she said, "with a dark red crescent on his neck, but you would know him best by the way he flies. He's very daring. He cuts the swiftest—"

The beaver stopped her. "Sorry. Haven't seen him."

"Perhaps you've heard his call, then, singing 'Bette.' "

No, the beaver shook his head.

"Or 'Rhone,' or 'Pavel'? They're our young."

Above, the gyrfalcon's head turned.

"They're just up the creek," said Bette.

With that, the falcon lifted her wings and dropped quietly from the limb.

She swooped behind the row of birch trees that lined the creek, weaving through the white stalks like a shadow. Then round the bend, she saw them: two chicks in a nest, baby sparrows on a low limb by the water.

Down she flew, in a smooth straight line for their tiny wriggling heads. She turned up her wings to brake against the air, then opened her sharp claws, but just as she was about to clamp them on the helpless little birds, there came a sudden blow from the right, and the falcon was struck to the ground.

She gathered herself as quickly as she could, and looked up in surprise. There before her was a reindeer, his antlers turned toward her purposefully, the fallen nest now safe between his legs.

"What's this?" she cawed. "Do I see right? Was that nest up in your antler?"

Caesar said nothing, but stayed poised above Pavel and Rhone—even as the falcon circled round to Ole and Gaino's sled.

"Well, aren't we a noble fellow?" She looked up and down the packages. "Not just playing daddy to a pair of sparrows, but bringing some things to a man-friend?

But what do you suppose they are?" She hopped up onto the hindmost package, the one with the bearskin cover, and took a peck.

"Stop," murmured Caesar, but the falcon paid no heed.

"I shall stop when you make me, reindeer." She took another peck. "The choice is yours: your little baby sparrows there, or this tasty sled of goodies."

Caesar growled, but the falcon only seemed to take pleasure at his predicament. She snipped again at the topmost package. The string flew up, and she was about to tear at the cover when out of nowhere Bette came swooping down and spiked her on the back. "Away! Away!"

The startled falcon squawked and flapped up to the nearest branch. "Well, well." She glared down at the two of them, and there was as much astonishment as anger in her eye. "Look at you two. Is this the mother, then? Is this your mate?" She shook her head disgustedly at Bette. "Do you call him deer or Mr. Sparrow?" She cawed at her own wit, then measured them both with a fierce black eye. "You'll answer for this, you two. You mark my words." She spread her wings. "You'll see." Then the falcon vaulted from her limb and sailed off into the woods—to wait on easier prey.

Bette stayed on Caesar's antler until the giant bird was gone from sight, then jumped down to the fallen nest. Pavel and Rhone both were trembling, frightened but fine.

"I'm sorry," said Caesar. "I didn't see until the last moment."

"Oh, no." She looked up at him. "No, I shouldn't have gone so far."

"Well, it won't happen again." Caesar turned down his head and hooked the nest back onto his antler. Bette found some more twigs to tie it fast again, and Caesar started off.

Not another word was said. All their hearts calmed down, Caesar's ankles clacked out their familiar rhythm, and soon enough Bette resumed her call for Piorello. But she never strayed so far from Caesar's antlers after that, and Caesar always kept an eye on the tree-line.

Seven

Piorello wasted no time trying to find his way home again. His first night at the school he spent in the corner of the girl's sill. She'd arranged a place for him to sleep by draping a soft red cloth over an abandoned robin's nest. He huddled there till dawn, then as soon as the sky cleared, he started off.

But it was a puzzle where to look. Normally, in his native wood, Piorello always had a good sense where he was, where the white house was, where the lake, where his nest. Home was a direction he'd simply always known and could turn any moment. But here, so far away, he'd lost his bearings entirely. He could sense it that very first flight, and he wasn't sure if it had to do with the bump on his head or being separated from the flock, but now as he flew from tree to tree, it was as if the hills around him were shifting and turning like the clouds.

He would not be daunted, though, and proceeded the only way he could. Starting that first day, Piorello began a survey of the countryside. He used the Seed Girl's sill as his home base, flying one mission after another, cautiously but steadily expanding his circle, in hopes as he progressed that at the very least he would gain a better sense of where he was, or—if he was lucky—that he might come across some clue, some sign that might help guide him home again.

Unfortunately, at least for the first few days, no such clue presented itself. But Piorello stuck to his plan. First thing each morning he'd go meet Bernard, the Saint Bernard, at the bench, and they'd head out to the meadows together. There were two, divided by a stream. Usually Bernard would stop on the near banks, but Piorello would fly out to the woods beyond, and down into the valley on the opposite side. Every day he flew just a bit farther, but the more he saw of the landscape, the more frustrated he began to feel.

The truth was, this place really wasn't so *unlike* home. If the mosses weren't quite as abundant, there was still a rich lawn, shagged by forests of trees he recognized, with the same needles and leaves and postures. Here, too, were waters of various moods—some still, some tidal, some running. Here were many of the same animals—other sparrows, jaybirds, blackbirds, bramblings, marsh tits, moles, voles, rabbits, and a host of others who were clearly kin to those he'd known at home. The ducks were the same, as were the swans, except for a thin black ridge they wore across their bills. He'd even found a scattering of cows out beyond the woods, and sheep—fatter here perhaps, but who still behaved much the same, grazing and mewing and lolling in the shade.

Really, the only difference between here and home seemed to be one of degree. That is, at least as he remembered, everything at home had seemed somehow more grand, more extreme. The hills, for instance, had all been so much steeper there. The lakes were wider. The sunlight had been warmer, the shade colder. The berries had slathered the slopes in much thicker drifts, and tasted more tart and more bitter. Even the bells that rang out through the countryside had somehow sounded louder at home, as if they yearned to meet the ridge of blue mountains that hung at the back of every glance, white-capped and spilling.

Here was no such majesty. Here it was as if everything took its lead from the groundsman's garden, so tame and reserved. Piorello searched high and low for something more—a steeper ridge, or a berry whose juice might pierce his tongue. If he'd found just one, then he might have known: This way. Follow here. But no. The fruit was mealy and mild. The bell tower whimpered, and the hills just kept rolling and rolling, a hue less green. He asked among the animals, but they were little help. The pigeons never offered so much as a coo in his direction. The squirrels were impossibly busy, and the house sparrows, for whom Piorello could well have been mistaken, acted as if he weren't even there. They were no better than the swans out on the pond, who, Piorello was eventually forced to conclude, simply did not speak at all.

No, the only one who talked to him was Bernard, who'd never ventured past the valley. So Piorello's only choice was to continue his search, each day flying that much farther, only to return to the sill that much more discouraged, that much more downhearted.

The one creature who kept him from feeling entirely hopeless and alone—other than Bernard, of course—turned out to be the girl, strangely enough. It hadn't been easy admitting it—he still resented her for sneaking him here—but now that they *were* here, now that they seemed to have settled, how could he deny her kindness? She always left two dishes out for him—one filled with seeds, the other with water. She tended to his nest. She even let him in when it was cold. There was a stone hollow in her room where she built fires in the evening, and she let Piorello sit beside it for as long as he liked. But she never closed him in. She always left the window open just a crack so he could come and go as he pleased.

He saw her a good deal, then, and soon came to realize not only that she was very kind, but that she wasn't particularly happy to be here either. He could see it in the mornings when she woke, the way she'd scold her socks as she pulled them on. Sometimes she'd come and sit with him at the window for a moment, and stroke his feathers, but always then the bells would ring. She'd sigh, kiss him goodbye, take up her burden of books, and go. By the time she emerged from the door below and started down the path, her head would have assumed a sullen tilt, as if a cloud were hanging over her and her alone.

Piorello would usually go meet Bernard then, and head off on his rounds, but often he would meet the girl again at the end of the day, out in the meadows. The girls all liked to come out in the afternoons and race around in bands, whacking a perfect little stone this way and that with sticks. But even there the Seed Girl seemed distracted. While the others tumbled over each other, she always seemed to be standing on the outside, starting and stopping, and chewing the ends of her hair.

That is, until she caught sight of Piorello. Then her face would light. She'd abandon her stick and go straight to him. And Piorello had to admit, it warmed his heart too, especially at the end of another fruitless day. They'd sit on the grass with Bernard until the bells called them in, then they'd all head back together.

Bernard would lumber off to his little swinging door, and Piorello would fly up to his sill. He'd have a quick meal and a bath, and the girl would come in not long after with her books and a new bundle of wood. She'd build a fire and change his dishes, and they'd spend the rest of their waking hours together— he, perched on the pencil in her pencil sharpener; she, hunched over her books, scrawling off endless jags of scribble.

Each day ended more or less the same. When the fire had turned to embers and the girl's eyelids had grown too heavy to lift, she'd push herself up and mark another large "X" on a great white leaf she kept pinned to the wall. Piorello would hop out to the sill, and the girl would pause a moment to kneel at her bedside. She'd take a shiny trinket from her drawer, and whisper something very faint to it, then close each night with the same odd gesture: touching her fingers to her forehead, then her chest, and then her shoulders, left to right.

Then she'd climb in bed and the light would die inside the room. Piorello would hunker down inside his soft red nest and look up at the stars. And he could never tell if it made him more happy or sad, their slow scroll across the sky, for of all the little ways this place was unlike home, the sky at night was the very same. It was the same black field behind, those were the same stars, that was the same moon. If only it could speak, thought Piorello, the moon could guide him back. The moon would know. But every night the moon held its tongue, so all Piorello could do was close his eyes again and hope—perhaps tomorrow he'd find something. Perhaps tomorrow, he could start back.

The day the girl turned over a fresh white leaf on the wall beside her desk, Piorello discovered his first real clue about where he was, and it wasn't very encouraging. He'd taken the morning to follow the little stream that glided through the meadows. He chased it all the way to a great open lake with rowboats and sailboats and fishermen. It reminded him of home almost, with the trees bordering the flat round enclave. But he'd flown to the top of a great pine tree to get a better view, and that is when he'd seen it, out beyond the bridge:

The sky and the water, and nothing between them. There it was again. The boundless blue lake.

He wasn't surprised, really—he'd known he would run into it eventually—but still, to see it there in front of him. He remembered from the journey over, when he'd tried to fly free from the girl, how quickly the wind had tossed him down, and so the sight of it now—the broad sky and blue horizon—caught in his throat.

He didn't stay long. He returned to the school soon after, stopping off at the groundsman's garden to gather his thoughts. He was on line at the apple-tree feeder when he happened to catch the eye of a robin in front of him. "Excuse me."

"What?" The redbreast turned his head peevishly.

"You wouldn't happen to know a direction I might be likely to find mountains?"

"Mountains?"

"Yes, you know—like the hills, but higher."

The robin didn't seem to know what he was talking about.

"Up in the clouds," he tried, "and with snow on top?"

"You mean in the winter?"

"Well, yes, in the winter, but all year. High."

The robin sputtered at the absurdity. "I don't know. Across the sea, maybe."

The sea. "Is that the giant lake out beyond the sailboats?"

"Yes," the robin tittered. " 'The giant lake.' "

"Yes, well, I'd actually prefer avoiding the sea if I could. You wouldn't know another way round?"

"Another way round." The robin looked at him as though he were a worm. "There isn't any way around, sillybeak. This is an *island*." He shook his head disdainfully and fled for the peg of the feeder.

An island. The word might have stabbed Piorello in the heart. There was an island back home, a lonely little mound out in the middle of the water. But that was so small, and this place was so large. What was he to do?

He was still there on his limb, trying to fathom the news, when Bernard came trotting in from the archway. "There you are, Piorello. Find anything today?"

"Bernard, did you know this was an island?"

"Nope." The big dog settled down beneath the tree. "Not sure what an island is."

"It means we're surrounded by water."

"Oh." He laid his muzzle down on his paws. "Well, that's something, I suppose."

Indeed, thought Piorello. A very discouraging

something. Surrounded by water, and spinning like a leaf for all he knew.

That night was the first heavy rain of the season. It started just after dinner. The girl brought in Piorello's things before they got too wet. She set his nest beside the fire to dry, and spread out the soft red cloth.

When time came for sleep, the rain was still fierce, so she left his nest where it was. That was the first night Piorello spent inside. As usual, the girl knelt a moment beside her bed, but then, after she'd turned out the light and climbed beneath her covers, Piorello noticed something he hadn't before—a sound she made in the dark, with her head pressed against her pillow. Fragile little gasps, a sniffling and a whimper.

So sad. Even with the rain beating against the window and the sky shuddering outside, he could still hear. She sounded the way he felt, and he knew it was true, what he'd suspected all along. The girl was no better off than he. She was trapped here, too.

Eight

As soon as Pavel and Rhone were strong enough, Bette taught them both to fly. The days were growing shorter. The slender stalks of all the birch trees, which shone so silver in the summer, now gleamed gold in the low sunlight. The weather was turning. Her young would need to know where to find seeds and water and how to fend for themselves.

So one morning, while Caesar paused for a drink of water, Bette nudged them both from the nest. "Come, come. Stand beside me. Perch." She showed them.

Pavel was first to respond. On wobbly legs he stepped from the nest onto Caesar's antlers.

"Now Rhone."

Rhone followed her brother awkwardly, but as soon as she was steady beside him, Bette flew up to the branch above them. "Now here."

The fledglings looked at her doubtfully, their wings hunched in dismay.

"Up!" she sang, but they still did not move. "Caesar." Caesar gave a quick toss of his head, and both Pavel and Rhone were suddenly thrown up into the air, so startled they barely managed to flutter their wings before falling back down to the antlers.

"That wasn't *too* bad," said Bette. "Now try again, but this time, remember to flap your wings."

Again Caesar tossed them up. The two young birds thrashed at the air, and this time, though once again Rhone dropped back down, Pavel actually ascended, up and up and then onto his mother's branch.

"Very good," she said.

Pavel was so impressed with himself, he puffed out his chest and gave his mother's call. "Piorello!" He shouted it to the forest triumphantly. "Piorello!" He looked down to his sister. "Come on, Rhone! Caesar, give her a toss!"

Caesar swung his head again, and Rhone flew up. Again, she beat her wings madly, and this time she, too, continued up, even hovering a moment before taking her place beside her mother and brother.

"Now call 'Piorello'!" said Pavel.

"Piorello!" she sang. "Piorello!" And her voice was so beautiful, so young and true, it seemed as though the forest fell silent to listen.

"That's very well done," said Bette. "Both of you. You see? Now you can fly. You may go wherever you like, to look for food and water."

"—and help look for Father!" said Rhone.

"Yes, that's right," Bette agreed, "and help look for Father."

"But what does he look like?" asked Pavel.

Bette thought, and was warmed by the idea. "Well, as a matter of fact he looks very much like you, Pavel. He has your colors, and a dark-brown crescent on his nape, but you'd know him best by the way he flies. He's very daring. He cuts the swiftest and most grace-ful arcs, but always lands with perfect poise."

Pavel took this as a challenge. He turned his eye on the next tree down and leapt straight off. He fell at first, nearly hitting the ground, but caught himself just in time to swing up and reach the lowest limb. "Piorello!" he shouted.

"Piorello," sang Rhone.

"Pio-rello," Caesar came trotting underneath. "Pio-rello, Pio-rello," he huffed.

The three birds looked at one another and couldn't help tittering at their friend's attempt at song, but they followed quickly after, singing high and long above him.

So Pavel and Rhone joined the search. They spent the rest of that day flying back and forth between the trees and Caesar's antlers, calling out their father's name. Bette showed them where to find seeds and how to bathe in the shallow creeks, and in the coming days they spent longer and longer stretches up in the canopy, while Caesar kept his steady pace below, weaving through the wood.

The third morning after taking wing, Pavel and Rhone were chasing one another up among the trees when Bette took a moment to rest on Caesar's antlers.

"They seem to be enjoying themselves," he said.

"*Piorello.*" Rhone's voice sounded from above. "*Piorello?*"

"Yes," Bette answered. "I remember when my brothers and I first learned to fly. I don't think we ever perched but to keep our balance."

"*Piorello?*" called Pavel.

Caesar waited a moment, just to make sure the wood held no answer. "You know," he said, but he stopped himself.

"What, Caesar?"

"Well." He seemed unusually hesitant. "I only want you to know, now that Pavel and Rhone can fly, you shouldn't feel you need to stay with me."

"Caesar." Bette was taken by surprise. "Do you not want us to stay with you?"

"No, it isn't that. But the lake is wider than I'd thought. I'm not exactly sure where my friends are, and the weather will be turning. I just thought you might need a warmer place than I can offer."

"You won't be taking shelter yourself?"

"No." He kept trotting. "From time to time, I suppose, but I'd like to reach my friends as soon as I can. Before the snow."

"Oh."

For a moment there was only the sound of his hooves crunching along the forest floor. Then finally Bette asked him: "Who are they, Caesar, your friends?"

She could feel his neck stiffen slightly.

"If you'd rather not say—"

"No. Their names are Ole and Gaino."

"Who?" Pavel landed beside his mother.

"Caesar's friends," said Bette. "The ones he's taking his gifts to."

Rhone alighted beside her brother. "Who is he taking his gifts to?"

"Ole and Gaino," said Pavel impatiently. "They're Caesar's friends."

"Reindeer friends?" she asked.

No, the antlers shook. "Men. Brothers, from a family who travel with my herd."

"And where is your herd?" asked Rhone.

"A long ways off."

"Why aren't you with them?"

"Because," Pavel huffed at his sister. "He has to take these things to Ole and Gaino."

Rhone still seemed puzzled. "But then why aren't *they* with the herd?"

Pavel had no answer for this. Nor, it seemed, did Caesar.

"Are they lost, too?" asked Rhone. "Like Piorello?"

"Maybe," said Caesar softly.

The children mulled this over. Pavel looked back at the sled. "And what are you bringing them?"

Again Caesar shook his head. "I don't know."

Pavel jumped back to the largest of the bundles, the one on the back seat with the darkest, thickest pelt. "You don't even know what this one is?"

"No." Caesar's eyes did not turn, his pace did not change, but Bette could tell he wasn't comfortable with the topic.

"All right, Pavel, that's enough. Come back up. Besides, there's something we need to discuss."

Reluctantly, Pavel flitted back to his sister's side.

Bette began. "I suspect you've both noticed the

days are growing shorter, and that certain trees are turning colors."

"Some are even shedding," said Pavel. "We saw them."

"Are they ill?" asked Rhone.

"No, they're not ill," said Bette. "They are preparing for the winter, just as we must. You'll see. Your feathers will be growing fuller, and Caesar's coat will thicken—because the winter's very cold, and there isn't as much food to go around. The rabbits will find their holes. The squirrels will find their hollows to store their nuts, and most of the birds will have to choose their winter homes as well."

Pavel and Rhone both nodded, but it didn't seem they understood what she was getting at.

"What I mean is that soon we may have to do the same, find a place to stay for when it's cold."

"What kind of place?" asked Rhone.

"Well, a tree, I suppose—"

"A tree?" Pavel seemed almost offended by the idea. "But what about Caesar?"

"Yes," said Rhone, "where will Caesar be?"

"Well, as he's just finished telling us, Caesar has to deliver these things to his friends, so he'll probably just keep on."

Pavel and Rhone took a moment to digest this. They looked as if they'd both just eaten a sour seed, then Pavel looked up. "But couldn't Father be up ahead?"

"Yes, " said Rhone. "He could even be with Ole and Gaino, couldn't he?"

Bette thought on it warily. "Yes, I suppose."

"Do you think so, Caesar?" Rhone looked down. "Might Father be with your friends?"

Click-clack click-clack. The antlers stayed very still as Caesar trotted on. "I think that would be very fortunate for your father."

"What if he is, Mother?"

"Yes, what if he is?" Pavel chirped. "I don't think we should leave Caesar."

Rhone shook her head in agreement.

"It will be very cold, though," said Bette. "You understand that?"

Pavel nodded. "If Caesar doesn't need to find a warm place, then neither do I."

"And me, too. I don't want to leave Caesar."

Bette looked at them both, and was filled with an unexpected sense of relief, and pride. "Caesar?" she called down. "Would you mind if we stayed?"

No, the antlers shook.

Rhone leaned over. "And we could even help you look for your friends. Would you like that, Caesar?"

His eyes turned up gently. "I don't think that's necessary yet, but thank you."

"We'll have to shore up the nest, though," said Bette. "It will get cold."

"You could use my velvet," offered Caesar.

Bette looked up to the tip of the antlers. The soft velvet cover was coming loose. She hopped up and gave it a tug.

"It doesn't hurt?" asked Rhone.

Caesar shook his head. Bette gave another pull, and the velvet peeled off, soft and thick. She flew it back down to the nest and tucked it inside the tangle of twigs and dried grass. "Well, thank you, Caesar. I think this will do fine. Pavel? Rhone?"

The two flew up and helped her with the rest, stripping Caesar's antlers and swaddling their nest in his velvet, to protect them from the coming cold.

PART IV

The Royals

Nine

The Seed Girl made a shroud for Piorello inside her room. She stood the limb of a small poplar in the corner underneath the sloped ceiling, and draped a linen over the top.

That was where he spent his nights now, in his nest underneath, but his sleep had been troubled. Ever since his trip to the boat-lake, he'd been having dreams about the sea—about being caught out in the middle, alone above the boundless blue water. With no land in sight, the wind would start tossing him back and forth. He'd feel his wings go powerless, and then he'd begin to fall, down and down toward the waves . . .

He'd always wake before he hit, but still that was no way to start the day, for he knew there was a real sea out there, waiting for him. Whichever direction he chose to go, the water and the sky were lurking, daring him to pass.

But then one morning, Piorello went to have a snack down in the groundsman's garden. He was helping himself to the fruit of a small cranberry bush, when he heard a familiar call from overhead—a honking, baying sound, which, before he could even give it a name, lifted his spirits.

He peeked out from the bush just in time to see: a flock of six geese gliding over the chapel. They were flying in formation, with a single bird at the helm, strumming his long wings and calling back in time, "Follow, follow."

Geese, thought Piorello. Geese would know.

Through the stone arches, he saw Bernard emerging from his door. "Bernard!" He flew over. "You didn't tell me there were geese."

"Well, only this time of year." The old dog seemed surprised by his interest.

"Where do they stay?"

"Oh, out by the bridge usually."

Piorello was off. He raced straight to the spruce,

from the spruce to the beech, and from the beech all the way out to the fields, where from the top of the white post he could see—there on the strand beside the stone bridge was a lone greylag goose, contentedly preening itself.

Piorello flew straight down and landed where the grass gave way to the flat mud of the bank.

He hopped up, but the goose was too occupied with his feathers to notice. "Excuse me."

The gander turned his eye.

"I'm sorry to interrupt, but I was wondering if I could have a moment of your time."

The goose took a seat on his soft belly and looked at him, mildly amused by the interruption. "Yes?"

"My name is Piorello. I've been staying over by the school with all the girls, but I'm from a forest very far away, and I thought I might have recognized your flock. Would that be possible?"

The gander turned his neck with pride. "It's certainly possible. Where are you from?"

"Well, that's the trouble, you see. I'm not sure. But it's a very beautiful place, with snow and mountains—"

The goose stopped him. "Perhaps if I heard your song."

"Oh. Yes, of course." Piorello puffed out his chest and sang, " *'Lo, Bette, 'lo. 'Lo, Bette, 'lo.*"

The goose listened, nodding, but not too surely. "I think I may have heard something like that. You're from across the water."

"Yes!" Piorello hopped. "Yes, that's right. Now, will you be going there again?"

The goose looked at him—this was an odd question. He shrugged. "When the time comes, I suppose. Why?"

"Well, I was thinking"—Piorello tried to calm himself—"if it were possible, I mean—" He paused again. He hadn't realized until now the awkwardness, the imposition, of what he meant to ask.

"Yes?" the goose prodded.

"Well. If perhaps you and your flock wouldn't mind my . . . coming along?"

The goose lifted his neck. This he hadn't expected. "With the flock?"

Piorello nodded.

At just that moment four geese appeared from round the river's bend, a mother and three goslings flying low and gently. In succession, they all untucked their feet. The mother and the first two landed smartly in the water, then the third, who was smaller, tumbled over in a great splash.

"Against the wind, dear, or that will happen every time." The mother turned and saw her mate had company. "Oh, excuse me."

"Celeste." The gander stood up. "This is . . . Piorello?"

"Yes," said Piorello. "Very nice to meet you."

"Celeste is my mate. I am Saire, and these are our goslings: Xander"—the eldest of the three, a very handsome young gander, tilted his head and glided off along the water; "Arvo"—the next oldest bowed her neck and did the same; "and Zoole"—the smallest and most brown gave a sweet nod from behind her mother.

"Very attractive." Piorello directed the compliment to Celeste. "I actually have a son and daughter as well, but I am afraid I haven't been able to see them since they first hatched."

"Piorello finds himself a ways from home," Saire explained. "And is wondering if he could come with us across the channel."

Celeste looked at Piorello in surprise. "Fly with us?"

Piorello nodded hopefully.

"Well." She turned to Saire. "I suppose we could ask Ado."

"Ado?" Piorello stepped up.

"The flock leader," said Saire.

The youngest, Zoole, looked round her mother again. "Ado has been leader ever since Mother and Father were goslings."

Saire turned to Celeste. "Is he still off with Gurnemanz's brood?"

"He was. But I think he came in early." She glanced over at the other side of the stream, where, tucked in a little semicircle of reeds, they could just barely see the hind of a lone goose.

"Oh. I didn't see him come in."

"Well, I don't want to bother him," said Piorello.

"No bother," said Saire. Across the stream, the feathers stirred faintly. "Looks like he's still awake. Come."

Just Saire escorted him. He floated across. Piorello waited till he'd nearly reached the other side, then whisked over himself, landing beside him on the far bank.

"Ado?" They both peeked round the reeds.

The great goose lifted his head from his tucked wings, and Piorello was stilled by the majesty of the bird who now turned his eye to receive him. "Yes?"

"Ado. This is Piorello."

Piorello stepped forward with a bow.

"He's wondering if he could come South with us this year. We thought he should speak to you."

The great bird shifted round to face them, then settled again. He looked down at Piorello with neither humor nor surprise, but a consideration both firm and gentle. "Where is your flock?" He spoke in a full, but slightly weary, voice.

"Back home. I am not from here."

Ado gave a faint nod. "But you think we can lead you back to them?"

"I hope."

"Have you ever migrated?"

"No."

"Hm." The goose thought, but gave no hint of either judgment or approval. "And I wouldn't suppose you've ever flown with geese."

"No, but I was thinking I could learn."

At this, Ado's eyes narrowed affectionately. "You understand we tend to cover rather long stretches at a time."

"I do, but I'm a good flier. You could ask the others in my flock, if they were here. I'm very quick and smart—"

"I'm sure you are," the great goose interrupted. "But it really hasn't to do with quickness, our way. It's more a matter of speed, and endurance."

"The crossing," Saire interjected.

"Yes." Ado returned a quick, stern glance. "You're aware there's a crossing?"

"Over the water, you mean? Yes, that's why I ask, in fact. I was hoping you'd help guide me to the other side."

"But you realize there would be no food and no rest."

"Yes."

Piorello could sense Ado's reluctance. It was understandable, and for a moment it occurred to him, the absurdity of his request. A sparrow flying with geese. But then he thought of Bette again, and Pavel and Rhone, and he refused to be daunted.

"Your Majesty. I don't mean to be an imposition. I just need to get home again. If it is a matter of crossing a sea, then I will cross a sea. All I ask is a lead. Just see me over, get me to the other side, and I will do the rest. It's just that I cannot wait here any longer."

The great goose looked down at Piorello now, his expression changed from one of concern to a warming admiration. "Do you mind my asking how you were separated from your flock?"

"No." Piorello was surprised by his interest, though. It was the first anyone had asked. "It was the day our two chicks hatched," he said. "I had gone to get some millet for Bette, my mate, but then I'd seen a flower I wanted to bring her instead. A white flower, like the one the Seed Girl had been wearing when we met. I was going to bring it back to our nest, but when I went to pluck it . . ." Piorello tried to think, but there it seemed the memory ended. "I'm not sure. Everything went blank, and the next I knew, I was trapped, and taken here." He shook his head. "I'm sorry, it doesn't make much sense to me either."

The goose pardoned his confusion with a nod. "Saire?"

Saire, who'd been observing their conversation only mildly, jolted up. "Sir?"

"Have you taken the goslings on their run this morning?"

"Yes. Celeste just came back."

"Would you mind next time if our friend Piorello came along?"

"Sir?"

Ado turned. "If he would like to fly with us, then he should see how we fly."

Piorello's heart rose. The leader was consenting.

Saire looked at him, a touch dismayed, then down at Piorello. "Of course."

"Oh, thank you!" Piorello turned back to Ado. "You've no idea what this means."

"Well, don't get your hopes too high. I should say, I'm not even sure we're going where you need, but we will be crossing"—he checked the sky—"another moon perhaps. Between now and then, you can practice. Then, when the time comes for us to leave, if you are still determined to come, of course you're more than welcome."

"Thank you, Your Majesty."

" 'Highness,' " he corrected with a weak smile, then gave a sleepy nod to dismiss them both.

"Very good." Saire started backing down the slope, and Piorello followed, bowing all the way to the water.

They crossed to the near bank again, where the rest of the family was still wading.

Piorello was beside himself with excitement. "To-morrow, then?"

"Yes," said Saire, still a bit dumbfounded. "In the morning."

"The morning." Piorello gave Celeste a nod as well, and the goslings, then started back across the mea-dow—his breast, for the first time in longer than he could remember, swelled slightly with hope.

The following morning, the geese were waiting for Piorello at the bridge.

"We were beginning to think you might not come," said Saire.

"Oh, no. I could hardly sleep." Piorello glanced across the water. Ado was still tucked inside the reeds. "Will Ado be joining us?"

"Not today," said Celeste. "He's still feeling a bit under the weather."

"Oh."

It was just as well Ado didn't come that day. Saire led them off to the boat-lake, as planned, and Piorello kept up well enough as long as the geese stayed to the river—he was able to skip along the tree-line beside them. But when they finally came to the lake, with its wide expanse, there he met with a good deal more trouble.

It was a blustery day, and the geese spent most of the morning crossing back and forth among the boats. Piorello was simply overmatched. He'd never fully appreciated the prowess of geese before, how broad and long their wings were, how fast and straight they could fly. Saire and Celeste could cruise from one side of the lake to the other, skimming the surface of the water the whole way. Why, compared to them, Piorello felt like a leaf in a storm, with his nubby wings, tossed this way and that. If it hadn't been for Zoole, the youngest— who hadn't so much trouble keeping up as a tendency to stray—Piorello would have lost them all entirely. As it was, he spent the morning darting frantically from boat to boat, and panting on their masts.

Saire and Celeste were both polite. They waited kindly for Piorello to catch up, and circled back to give silent encouragement, and when at midday the group of them finally returned to the bridge, Saire made sure to invite Piorello back. "We'll be going every morning. You're more than welcome."

Piorello was simply too tired and embarrassed to reply. He thanked them all with a silent nod and left, hopping the whole way back to the buildings, his little wings were so exhausted.

That afternoon he took a long nap instead of a meal, but shortly after he woke up, he went to the groundsman's garden to snack on grass-seed. He'd been rethinking the morning's ordeal, trying to bolster his confidence again, when through the arches he heard an unexpected voice.

He didn't recognize it at first, but one of the geese was calling his name. He fluttered through the arches to see that it was Zoole, the youngest, standing in the cross-paths of the quadrangle. One of the sisters was sitting beside her, trying to get her attention with a crust of bread, but the little goose was looking up at all the windows, honking, "Piorello?"

"Zoole." He flew over. "What are you doing here?"

"Xander and the others are going on a chase. Do you want to come?"

Piorello was so surprised, and touched, he couldn't refuse. "All right," he said. "Thank you."

And so they went, as unlikely as it may have seemed. Zoole led Piorello back over the meadows and up the river this time, all the way to the small pond where the swans sometimes liked to wade.

It actually wasn't so small. It only seemed so, because of all the reeds. They covered nearly half the surface. Zoole landed at the outside edge and floated in. Piorello hopped beside her from stalk to stalk. They could hear the cousins deep inside, and followed the sound of their voices to a small clearing in the middle.

Xander and Arvo were there, and Zoole introduced the others—Gregory, Gerdes, Tim, Persimmon, and Goliath.

"Piorello is from over the water," Zoole announced brightly.

"Really?" The goslings all gathered round.

"What's it like?" asked Gerdes. "Is it as beautiful as Mother and Father say?"

"You've never been?" Piorello looked among them, but they all shook their heads—all but Xander, who seemed a touch impatient. "Oh, it is beautiful," said Piorello. "They're right."

"Father says there's golden berries," Persimmon spoke up.

"Oh, there are all kinds of berries, but yes, there are golden berries, too."

"And what else?"

"Yes, what else?"

"Well, there are white trees."

"White trees!" Arvo explained. "Can you imagine, Xander?"

"There are white trees here," her brother replied sourly. "You've seen them, out by the regatta."

"Yes," said Piorello, "that's true, but where I come from, there are whole forests of them, growing on mountainsides."

"Mountainsides?"

"Yes. The land there rises higher than Ado flies, and the peaks are all topped with snow."

"Snow." Persimmon sighed. "Sounds beautiful."

"I can't wait," said Arvo, and the cousins all shook their heads in wonder, all again but Xander.

"Look, are we going to talk, or are we going to play?"

"Play," concurred Tim. "Who's It?"

"Xander. Xander won last."

"All right then," Xander looked at Piorello. "The one who's It hides. That's me. The rest of you see if you can find me."

"And he can move if he wants," said Goliath.

"And no one flies above to see," said Gerdes. "That's cheating."

"It's not cheating," said Xander. "You can do whatever you want. You've still got to catch me, and you won't unless I let you." He gave them each a look of pity, then flew off into the golden labyrinth.

Zoole floated over beside Piorello. "Now wait." All the cousins were quiet, listening, then from deep inside the reeds came Xander's call: "Good luck . . . ducks!"

That got them going. The birds all flew off in pursuit, Piorello too. They raced through all the little passageways, splitting up and shouting out to each other, but Xander was right. He proved an elusive target, taunting them, calling from behind the bushes and disappearing, luring them here and there, but never giving himself away.

Never, that is, until Piorello finally decided to give chase. The game had lasted long enough. Some of the cousins were beginning to complain, so the next time he heard Xander—teasing his sister Zoole back near the meeting place—Piorello raced directly there and caught him from behind, much to everyone's surprise but his own.

Piorello turned out to be an excellent player, in fact. This was a game much better suited to his talents. He was quicker than they. He could dart around corners and surprise them whenever he liked. His turns as It lasted far longer than anyone else's, even Xander's, but none of the cousins seemed to mind, as they'd never known an adult—even such a small adult—to come and play with them.

Piorello had enjoyed himself as well. It was fun speeding through the reeds and routing out the goslings, but then very late in the afternoon something happened—something which in a matter of moments rescued all the hopes that the morning's run had very nearly dashed.

The second-to-last round, Arvo's turn had come as It. The cousins were all sweeping through the reeds looking for her, and Piorello was following behind Xander, as he was the most cunning of the cousins. At one point, Xander decided to take a spin above the pond to see if he could spy his sister's hiding place. Just a few strums of his broad wings and he was well above the golden labyrinth—but what was so surprising, so uplifting, was that Piorello was swept right along in Xander's wake. He had been trailing so close behind that he too found himself high up above the reeds.

But what a sensation! Piorello had drafted behind other birds before. He'd done it all the time back at home, with other sparrows, but never as large a bird as a goose. He'd never experienced anything like it. They circled high above the others. How small the trees looked from up there, how downy the reeds, but it was the speed that Piorello found most thrilling, and the stillness of the air. Why, if I could fly like this, he thought, just stay inside the geese's wake, I could fly from here to anywhere, across any old sea.

Of course, no sooner did he think this than Xander caught sight of his sister's hiding place. He turned down so quick that Piorello lost hold. The high wind gave him a brisk swat for being so bold, and he had to spiral back down to the reeds, as the buffeting breezes permitted.

Still, in just that brief tour above the pond, he'd felt it: there definitely was a chance. There was a way.

He played the remainder of that round and then one more, then they all adjourned for the day. Piorello did not tell the goslings of his discovery, but promised he'd be back tomorrow. Zoole said she'd come and get him, and the cousins all agreed, even Xander. They'd be happy to have him come and play.

But none was near as happy as Piorello. None had so much to gain. Leave the parents to their training runs out on the lake. Piorello would practice with the goslings.

Ten

The change had been gradual, but the darkness was settling in now. Caesar had passed beyond the lake. The forest was deep all around them, but there was still no sign of Piorello or Caesar's friends, and Bette could tell he was growing anxious. He was stopping more often, peering through the trees and checking the sky, which had grown much more moody lately—now mild, now cold, now hazy, now clear.

But it was twilight. They were following alongside a creek when Pavel called down from a treetop. "Mother, look!"

"What?" Her breath caught.

"The sky."

Bette turned up and saw it too, drifting down gently like white feathers.

"It's beautiful," said Rhone. "What is it?"

"Snow," Bette answered. She could feel Caesar's head shake quietly beneath her and she knew why: they had not beat the winter. Caesar's friends were still deep inside the wood, and now the snow was here.

The storm developed quickly. The flakes grew in size and number, sticking to all the leaves and needles. "Come. Inside the nest."

They all climbed in together, but even there, they could hear the wind beginning to howl, the snow patting down around them, clinging to their velvet cover, sealing them in.

"Do you think Caesar's all right?" asked Rhone.

"Of course he is," said Pavel.

Then suddenly the wind fell off. They'd stopped.

Bette looked out. "Caesar?"

"We'll wait here for a while."

They were standing in the mouth of a small cave. Bette could barely see beyond the opening. It was a full-fledged blizzard.

Pavel poked his head out. "Where are we, Mother?"

"A cave." Their voices echoed faintly.

"Can't stay long, though." Caesar pulled the sled beneath the canopy. "The snow will trap us."

Pavel and Rhone both jumped to the ground. "What's a cave?" asked Rhone.

"Just the insides of a hill," answered Bette.

Pavel peered inside. "How far does it go?"

"Depends," she said. "Some are deep. Some not."

"Do you think Father might be here?" Rhone called into the darkness, "Piorello?"

The shadow was still. There was just her voice, bouncing down the stony walls.

"I don't think so," said Bette. "But don't worry, we won't stay long." She looked back outside. There was a smooth branch stuck in the ground beside the entrance. "We'll go when the snow gets halfway up that stick."

"Stick?" Caesar's head snapped up, then suddenly he became stone still.

"Caesar, what is it?"

"Shshshsh—" With a jerk of his head Pavel and Rhone both flew up to his antlers.

"What?" whispered Bette.

He nodded toward the stick and spoke low. "Bear. The men plant those outside their dens."

Bette looked back into the cave, breathless, and the children began inching their way along the antlers to her side.

"Do you think he's asleep?" she asked.

"Don't know."

"Mother." Pavel was right next to her. "What's a bear?"

"The king of the forest," she whispered.

The children both peered into the black for some sign of this creature, but the shadow was too dark and deep to see.

"What's he look like?" asked Pavel.

"He's very big."

"Bigger than Caesar?"

"Yes. He has dark fur like the last gift on the sled. And big paws."

"Teeth?"

"Yes."

"Sounds ugly," said Pavel.

Caesar shook his head.

The birds all kept searching the darkness, then Rhone spoke. "What makes him the king?" she asked.

Bette thought. It was a good question, what made the bear king. She didn't know. Then came Caesar's voice, soft and low. "He is no one's prey but man's."

The children both nodded vaguely, but then Rhone asked, "What's prey?"

"It means he can eat whatever he likes," said Pavel. "Right, Mother?"

Bette nodded. "Shshshsh."

Rhone's eyes were wide. "What does he like?"

"Fish." Bette waited for the wind to cover her voice. "And nuts and berries."

"And honey," added Caesar.

"Yes, and honey."

A moment passed, then Rhone spoke again. "Ever birds?"

Bette was silent. Again, she wasn't sure.

"Birds?" Rhone asked again.

"Yes, birds," snipped Pavel. "If he can have whatever he likes, then he can have birds. Right, Caesar?"

Caesar nodded faintly. "If he likes."

There was another, longer silence now, which once again only Rhone had the nerve to break. "Ever reindeer?"

"Rhone, hush," said Caesar. "He can choose whatever he likes, but he and his family like to slumber through the winter. If we let him sleep, he won't harm anyone."

With that, Bette nudged Pavel and Rhone back toward the nest. "Come. Inside."

Pavel was the more reluctant. "But you'll tell us if he comes out?"

"I will, but he won't. Now quiet." She nudged them both over the lip, then fluttered in herself.

It was a while before Pavel and Rhone fell asleep

that night. Bette could feel their hearts thrumming in the dark, but finally the warmth of the nest and the faint sway of Caesar's breathing subdued them. Bette tucked them in beside each other, and quietly climbed back out.

Caesar was still facing the storm, but with his ears turned back. "Are they asleep?"

"Yes."

They looked out together. The snow was still falling thickly. The ground was covered. The pines were draped in white. It was as if autumn had never been.

"Caesar?" Bette whispered. "You said the bear was no one's prey but man's?"

"Yes."

"Man eats the bear?"

"Yes. Sometimes."

"Your friends?"

"Yes."

The snow gave a howl. She hadn't expected this of Caesar's friends. "They eat whatever they like?"

Caesar nodded faintly.

"They must be strong," she said.

"Smart."

"Oh."

That was the last they spoke, but Bette spent the

rest of the night out with Caesar, listening for the sound of the bear behind them, and watching the snow blanket the forest, and climb the stake.

It never did reach halfway. The storm let up just before dawn, and Caesar pulled them out into the white.

Pavel and Rhone awoke soon after, and their eyes sprung wide when they lifted their heads and saw.

"What happened?" asked Pavel.

"It's only the snow," said Bette.

Rhone looked up at a passing birch, stripped of leaves.

"And the wind."

The young sparrows both nodded gamely, but Bette could see they were scared, and she didn't blame them. Just yesterday, they'd been trotting through an autumn forest, fleet and rife with life. But they'd awakened to an entirely new world, bare and white and quiet. The only sound was the crunch of Caesar's hooves tramping through the snow, and the halting hiss of the runners behind them.

Caesar tried to cheer them. As soon as he reached a flat-enough stretch, he struck a rhythm and started up his huffing and puffing accompaniment to the sparrows' song—"Pio-rello, Pio-rello, Pio-rello." But the birds did not join in. It was hard to imagine Piorello in this new place.

"That's all right, Caesar," said Bette finally. "You don't have to."

"Would you prefer I not?"

"Maybe."

And so they went in silence, Pavel and Rhone gaping at the transformed wood, while Caesar struggled knee-deep through the winter's first blanket.

Eleven

Piorello went about his days much differently now. He didn't go on his rounds anymore. He was committed to flying with the geese. The geese would take him home. Now he used the mornings to rest up and prepare for his afternoons, which he spent almost entirely with the cousins out at the reeds.

For the cousins, of course, it was all fun and games—to race and play chase and hide-and-seek—but for Piorello, these afternoon competitions were much more important than that. For Piorello, they were training, a chance to work on the skills he would need to make it across the sea. Every chance he got, he'd swing behind the geese and practice flying in their wake. When they held their races, he'd tag along behind for as long as he could. Soon he was able to draft from one side of the pond all the way to the other, like a little ribbon tied to their tail feathers. The other animals at the pond were even beginning to take notice. The squirrels and the ducks would watch him whistle by and remark to one another how they'd never seen a sparrow fly so. "Talented bird." "And determined," they'd agree. Even the swans would nod their heads in admiration. Piorello saw them, and it began to seem like not such a mad idea, his flying with Ado's flock.

Every night he returned to his room, exhausted but hopeful. While the girl hunched over her books, scribbling, sometimes he couldn't help himself. He'd perch next to her and sing, "I think I may be going, you know. I'll be leaving with the geese soon."

But she would only put her finger to her lips.

"You could come, too, if only you could fly. We'd take you as well."

But "shshshsh" was all she'd say, and then turn back to her endless scribbling.

Then one drizzly afternoon, Zoole's call failed to come. Piorello waited on the sill as usual, but when the bells rang three and still there was no word, he wondered if something was the matter.

He made his way out to the bridge. From the white posts he could see that the whole family was there—Saire, Celeste, and the goslings. Piorello approached from as high as he could, circling the river over and back several times before landing on the strand.

"Very impressive," said Saire.

"I've been practicing."

"So the young ones tell us."

Piorello looked over at Xander, who seemed unusually grumpy. "Good afternoon, Xander."

"Afternoon," he answered glumly, then floated off, glaring at his reflection.

"Is something wrong?" Piorello turned to Saire and Celeste, and he could tell there was. They seemed very uncomfortable all of a sudden.

"Actually," said Saire, "there is something."

Celeste cut in. "We know the work you've been doing, and probably we shouldn't even worry you, but I think you should know. Saire and I and some of the parents have been talking, and there is a possibility . . . a *possibility* we may not be going."

"Not going?" Piorello looked at her. "But why?"

Celeste took a deep, almost repentant, breath. "Well, it seems Ado isn't feeling very well—"

"We think he may have eaten a bad mushroom," said Saire. "I'm sure he'll be fine, but some of us were thinking that if he isn't better in time for the migration, perhaps we'll stay the winter."

Piorello was stunned. He looked across the water. He could see Ado had tucked himself even further inside his nook. "But what about when it gets cold?"

Saire nodded. "Ado has told us that his father's flock used to spend the winter here sometimes, and that it wasn't so bad." He directed the statement at Zoole and Arvo, who were still floating beside them. "It gets its share of rain and snow, but the river never turns to ice. That's the important thing."

Arvo was not consoled. She bowed her head and floated out after her brother.

"I am sorry, Piorello." Celeste was looking at him with such sympathy. "We just thought you should be aware."

"No. Thank you." He tried not to show his disappointment. "You certainly can't go without Ado."

"And it all might work out fine," said Saire. "He could feel perfectly well tomorrow."

"Yes," Piorello answered softly. "Yes, of course." The two older goslings were over beneath the bridge now. "In the meantime, I suppose all I can do is keep flying."

Celeste nodded. "I'm sure the children would enjoy that. They are so fond of you, Piorello."

"And I am fond of them." He turned to Zoole. "You'll come and get me if you go to the reeds?"

"Yes."

"All right, then." He looked at them all for an awkward moment, then he said good day and left.

The cousins did not play that afternoon, but even if they had, Piorello doubted he would have joined them, he'd been so upset by this news.

He did go the next day, but they didn't play very hard or stay as long. Piorello could tell just from the lilt of Xander's wings that Ado was no better, and when he escorted the goslings back to the bridge at dusk, he could see for himself. The old bird was still inside his nook, unmoved.

And there he remained. Days passed, one to the next. Other flocks began to leave. Bramblings. Blackbirds. Even some geese. But Piorello kept waiting on Ado, practicing with the goslings in the afternoons, and then returning to the bridge every night, only to find their leader still there, in the same spot he'd been the day before, and the day before that.

The only hope he took was in the presence of the geese on the opposite strand. Every day, it seemed there were more. The parents all were gathering in the

114

long, cold shadow of the bridge to wait for Ado. As long as they were there, Piorello had to believe there was still a chance. What he feared was returning one evening to find them gone, off somewhere looking for winter nests.

Twelve

There were no more blizzards like the first. It snowed some, but not as hard, and the winds never mustered quite the same bite. During the few daylight hours, Bette and the children moved back to their perches on Caesar's antlers, but they didn't sing as much. Every so often they'd pass by a rabbit hopping through the snow, or a squirrel emerging from its hollow for a breath of air, but most of the animals seemed to have turned in for the winter, and more than ever it seemed the forest was theirs and theirs alone.

Then one clear morning, Caesar slowed to a stop

in a copse of tall birches and began looking around.

"What is it, Caesar?"

"Nothing." He looked behind. "I just thought Ole and Gaino might be here."

"Piorello?" called Rhone. "Piorello?"

Bette took a look round herself. She peered over the ridge, and her breath caught.

Standing out in front of them, looking back at her and grinning, was a lone wolf with ice-blue eyes.

"Caesar," she whispered, "go."

He'd seen, too. He started again, calmly and at the same pace as before.

"Pavel, Rhone, look straight ahead. Say nothing." Bette gathered them to her side, but she could hear the wolf coming up behind them now, sniffing the air curiously.

"Well, well, well," he sniggered, "could it be? Three little birds, a reindeer, and a sled. Yes, I think I may have heard of you." He came trotting up alongside. "You must be Pavel, and you Rhone."

Bette looked down in alarm. "How do you know their names?"

"Oh, we've an acquaintance in common." The wolf smiled. "You remember the falcon. She told us of the little errand your friend here was running." He turned his icy eyes up at Caesar. "Didn't get his name, though. Mr. Sparrow, was it?"

Caesar did not respond. He continued on as if the wolf were not there.

"Tsk, tsk, tsk." The wolf shook his head. "The men do cast a spell on the reindeer, don't they? Makes one wonder. Any idea what we might be bringing them?"

"Why don't you leave us alone?" Pavel chirped down.

"Oh, it's only that I'm curious, little one. Aren't you? To know why your friend should have come so far afield?" He sniffed the air. "Yes, I think I can even smell it." He looked back at the sleigh.

Caesar picked up his pace now, but then out of nowhere three more wolves appeared behind the line of birches, trotting along and looking over at them with grinning, dripping mouths.

"Mmmm, yes." The white-eyed wolf kept up, his nose above one of the middle packages on the sled. "This one smells tempting." He pawed at the bundle, and Caesar broke into a gallop.

The sparrows were tossed up into the air, and the three dark wolves raced out ahead to block Caesar's path. He lowered his antlers to charge, but just as he was about to break through the line, the white-eyed wolf pounced on the sleigh from behind. The blades sunk fast, the reins jerked, and Caesar was yanked back.

"Caesar!" called Bette, but the three snarling wolves

were upon him. The first he threw against a tree with a quick swipe of his antlers, but the second attacked from the rear. "Behind!" called Pavel, but too late, the wolf clamped him by the neck. Caesar reared up on his hind legs to shake him loose, but the wolf held fast.

Suddenly Pavel shot down and stabbed him in the eye. The wolf fell off howling, and Caesar lunged at the third, but he was still outnumbered. In a flash, the wolves were surrounding him again. They held their positions, waiting for word from their leader, who was standing back from the sled now, the middle package between his legs.

"Leave it," murmured Caesar.

"Sorry?" The wolf chuckled. "Didn't hear."

"That's not for you."

"Not for us? But aren't we your friends, too? Don't you want us to eat this winter?"

The three wolves closed in. They wanted more. Caesar lowered his antlers to ready himself. For a moment, they all stood poised, but finally the white-eyed wolf called them off.

"Oh, don't bother," he said. "Let the men have their goodies." The others backed away slowly. "And don't worry too much about your man-friends—Caesar, was it? They'll make do, I'm sure." The wolf smiled. "They can always eat you." He sniffed the bundle. "From the smell of this, I'd say they'll be only too happy."

119

The dark wolves all sniggered as the white-eyed leader took the bundle in his jaws and began dragging it away through the snow, back into the woods for a pack feast.

Caesar watched until they were over the ridge and safely away, then Bette flew down. "I'm sorry."

Caesar said nothing. His eyes were grave, his chest still heaving from the battle.

"At least they didn't take everything." Rhone flew down to the sled, to the large bundle on the hind seat. "This one's here. That's good."

Caesar nodded. "What about the nest?"

Bette checked. It had been smashed on one side. Some of the velvet had come undone and was dangling—but then she saw his right brow antler. One of the tines had broken off. "Oh, Caesar!"

"Can we put it back on?" Pavel was already down in the snow, right beside where the broken tip spiked the white surface.

"Leave it," said Caesar. "The nest?"

"Easily fixed. Pavel? Rhone? Come and help."

Caesar took a step to leave, but the sled seemed to tug at him. One of the straps had broken off.

"Will you be all right?" asked Bette.

"It's just the one," he said, and he started again. Bette didn't know where for—wasn't even sure if Caesar knew, or why he should be so kind to these men, Ole and Gaino. She'd heard what the wolf had said. But Caesar didn't even hesitate. Off they went, the silence of the forest now disrupted by the scuffing of the sled runners as they scuttled askew across the snow.

Thirteen

The autumn had been mild, but winter arrived right on schedule. The twelfth of December brought the first real frost. Elsbeth was awakened by the sound of one of her books crashing down from the windowsill. Even from her bed she could feel the air whistling through the crack.

She put on her robe and slippers and scampered over. The bird met her at the sill. He'd been wakened, too.

"Good morning," she said, holding her elbows and

shivering. "You know what this means? Means we'll be leaving soon, going to London. For Christmas."

The bird didn't seem to care one way or the other. He was perched on the sill, peeking out. She moved to close the sash. "Do you want to go?"

She lifted it just a touch for him, and he hopped underneath.

"All right," she spoke down through the gap. "Just call when you come back, because I have to close the window now. All right?" She looked down through, but the sparrow was already gone, headed out to the fields as usual.

Before she lowered the sash, she went and got his bowls and set them outside on the ledge, just in case he came back early.

. . .

Piorello made straight for the geese. The frost was here. Today. If they were going to leave, they'd do it today. That or begin finding their winter nests.

From the meadow spruce he could see them, though, all sleeping along the strand. They were a curious sight. There must have been two dozen now, all pointed in the same direction, and lined up in the same formation as they liked to fly.

Piorello whisked down and landed among them, but no one stirred. It was disturbing, the depth of their slumber. He hopped from one to the next. Their heads were all tucked, and there was a light dusting of snow on their backs.

Saire and Celeste were up near the front. Piorello stopped in front of them, but they didn't budge.

Then from behind came a groggy young voice.

"Piorello." It was Zoole, smiling, just lifting her head.

"Hello, Zoole."

"Mother, wake up, it's Piorello."

Celeste stirred, and lifted her head drowsily. "Oh. Good morning, Piorello."

"Morning. I'm sorry to bother you, but I just thought you should know—the frost is here."

"Is it?" Her whole body shivered as if to shake loose the grip of sleep. She consulted the sky. "Yes, I suppose it is."

"Does that mean you're staying, then?"

She looked back at him, and her expression turned. "Oh, Piorello. I'm sorry."

"No. It's all right." He didn't want her to feel bad. He glanced at the vacant patches behind her. "Do you know where Xander and Arvo are?"

Celeste shook her head. She still seemed oddly disoriented. "The reeds, I'd imagine."

"Are you going?" asked Zoole.

"I thought I might. See how they're doing."

"Can I go, Mother?"

"Of course. Just don't be too long." She set her head back down. "You don't want to fall behind." Her eyes closed gently, and she was asleep.

Piorello wasn't sure what she'd meant, but he and Zoole headed off quietly. They flew side by side along the river to the reeds, touching down at their usual entrance.

They could hear the group of them somewhere near the middle—Xander, Arvo, and the cousins—but as they came near, it was Xander's voice that rose above the others. He was whispering, but he sounded so angry that Zoole and Piorello both paused behind the nearest row of reeds to listen.

"No, it isn't fair," he was saying. "Mother and Father got to go when they were young."

"Yes, and so did mine." It was the voice of one of the cousins. "They never had to stay."

"You think if they asked Ado, he'd want us to stay?"

"No."

"No, of course not."

"He'd say go."

"Of course he would."

Piorello was watching Zoole. At first she seemed confused by what she heard, then disturbed. She looked back at him a moment before starting round the reeds herself.

"Zoole." Xander saw her first. "Where did you come from?"

"From the strand. You're not thinking of going, are you?"

Piorello could see through the reeds, the cousins were all looking down at the water, except for Xander. "Yes," he said.

"But why?"

"Because—we're tired of it here, Zoole. Aren't you? Don't you want to see?"

"But we'll see."

"No, Zoole, we won't. Mother said we're not going."

"But we are," she insisted. "We left last night."

The cousins were silent a moment. They looked at one another, puzzled, then finally Xander spoke. "Zoole, what are you talking about?"

"Don't you remember?" She glided to their midst. "We started last night. Just now. Ado was out in front, and Mother and Father were up on the right. We've started already."

Xander shook his head. "You were dreaming, Zoole."

"No," she said. "It wasn't a dream. It was just now. The sky was all white, and we were singing. We just passed from the land to the sea, and we were calling."

126

She looked at her sister. "You remember, Arvo. We saw the water up ahead, and you and I were singing."

Arvo looked back at Zoole. She'd seemed as baffled as the others at first, but now there was a glint of recognition in her eye. "I do remember something."

"Yes, a dream," Xander broke in. "You know that, Arvo. Ado isn't taking us anywhere. You can go back right now and see for yourself."

"He is, too," insisted Zoole, "and I don't think you should talk that way."

"I'm not saying anything wrong. I'm just saying Ado isn't going anywhere, and if you keep pretending to follow him, then neither will you."

Xander paused. He looked around at the circle of cousins. Their heads were still bowed—all except for Zoole, who was looking back at him with the same expression of certainty and concern.

"Well." He shook his head. "I'm not going to make any of you go. You can stay if you like, but the next geese I see, I'm leaving. Any of you want to come along, fine. If you don't, fine. But I'm not staying here in the cold." He looked directly at Zoole. "And let me tell you something else"—he leaned toward her with an almost menacing glare—"you cannot tell Piorello."

"Why not?"

"Because. Piorello will tell Mother and Father."

"No, he won't."

"Yes, he will, or he's going to want to come along."

"So?"

"So? Zoole, he's a sparrow. You've heard Father. Just because he can cross a river, just because he's learned to circle the reeds doesn't mean he can keep up during the crossing. Plus, Father doesn't even think we're going in the right direction. He says Piorello has to go all the way up North."

Zoole was looking at her brother now as if he'd injured her.

"Listen to me." His voice softened. "I like Piorello. I wish he could come, but none of us have ever been, and I'm not going to be the one responsible for taking him. Not alone. Do you understand?"

"Yes," she answered meekly.

"And you're not going to tell him?"

"No."

Piorello didn't wait to hear the rest. He left silently from behind the reeds, weaving low through the islands, so he would not be seen.

He did not return to the room right away. He didn't want to see the girl just yet. He went to the groundsman's garden and found a perch inside a cranberry bush to think.

Maybe Xander was right. Maybe there had never

been a chance. He looked out at the garden, and for the first time he wondered if this was to be his home forever.

The groundsman was out. He was digging up the bulbs that lined the walks, scattering pine needles on the flower bed, and covering the rosebushes with coarse sacks. The garden would be sleeping soon, like all the geese, and Piorello didn't know if he could bear it—the thought of another season here, a winter here without Bette.

Then, from through the arches, he heard Zoole's voice, calling his name.

He fluttered over and found her at the bench. "Zoole, you didn't have to come. In fact, you probably shouldn't have."

She shrugged. "I don't care what Xander says."

"But you should. Your brother's right."

"He's not." She looked at him, still so innocent and sure. "We *are* going, and you could come, too. That's what I came to tell you. If you wanted, I'm sure Ado would let you."

"That's a dream, Zoole. You should listen to your brother."

Zoole only shook her head.

Just then the bells began to ring. "I should probably go," she said. "You won't tell Mother and Father—about Xander."

"No."

"Thanks." She paused. The girls were beginning to emerge from the doors. "I'm sorry, Piorello."

"It's all right. I'll see you, Zoole."

Zoole spread her wings and left.

The Seed Girl was coming over now, calling out to him. She offered her hand, and without thinking, Piorello took it. She brought him inside, up the two flights to her room. His room, with the window still closed.

.   .   .

For two days, the cold wind shuddered against Elsbeth's window and teased the shutters from around the cracks. Still, each morning she gave her bird a chance to go out. She'd lift the sash for him and wait, but he didn't seem to want to anymore. He just sat on the poplar limb, puffed up and silent.

She could tell he was unhappy. She brought him treats, but he ate little, and slept much. Every so often he'd come down for water or to look outside the window, but there wasn't much to see now. The squirrels and sparrows had all staked out their dwellings in the trees, and there wasn't a murmur in the sky. All the flocks were gone, or were sleeping somewhere sound. So the bird would return to his limb, quiet and forlorn.

Finally, the holiday was upon them. The night before they were to leave, Elsbeth got her things ready.

She took out all her warmest clothes, and set them in piles on her bed, and she spoke to the bird as she folded them.

"Don't worry," she said. "Just one more night. And London's not so bad." She kept saying it over and over—"London won't be so bad"—every new blouse or sweater she folded. She took down her hatbox and set her dolls inside. And she told them, too. "It won't be so bad." But they just sat in their circle, silent, waiting for tomorrow, waiting for the locket and for the sparrow to make the journey with them.

. . .

His third day inside, Piorello was awakened by the girl's voice coming from the window. He hopped down to see. The light coming in was gleaming bright, and the panes were grinning with snow.

Piorello jumped to the top of the sash. Down below, the quadrangle was white. A thin silver crest topped all the limbs, roofs, and fence posts. The groundsman was shoveling the walk, and everywhere the girls were leaning out their windows, calling to one another excitedly.

But what about the geese? thought Piorello. Had they found their winter nests in time?

Right then the girl pulled up the sash to look outside, and out flew Piorello, into the cold.

He could hear her call after him. She cried for him

to come back, but he didn't even turn. He raced for the fields as fast as he could, from the spruce to the bath to the post.

The white was everywhere, blanketing both meadows, but he could still see the little stream dividing them, the stone bridge crossing, and, there on the near slope, what looked like a garden of gray stones.

He flew down and landed among them. Just their backs were showing through the snow. He hopped up to the pair at the front. "Celeste? Saire?" He pecked at the feathers, but they were frozen stiff. All of them, it looked like—the entire flock.

Or maybe not all. Just behind he saw several faint imprints, and for a moment he took heart—the goslings had gotten away. But then he noticed a little brown hump in their midst, just barely showing through.

"Zoole?"

He hopped over. "Zoole? Is that you?" He swept away the snow which had settled against her neck and head. "Zoole, wake up." But his friend lay motionless, her eyes frozen shut.

No, thought Piorello. No, it can't be. He peered across the icy stream, at the little nook where Ado lay, his back cresting the white cover. Oh, look what you have done! he thought. Look where you have led them!

The wind hissed across the plain. A silver cloud of

132

snow-dust swirled down from the rail of the bridge, and suddenly it was too much. Piorello climbed from Zoole's back and lay his tiny body down against her cold, hard feathers. He wished he'd never wakened in the girl's nest. He wished he'd never seen this terrible place.

He closed his eyes and thought of all the geese, just as Zoole had said—all flying in formation, with Ado out front, the sun up above, and the blue sea below. He thought of them all calling as they flew, further and further away, and he wished for the snow to come and bury him as well.

PART V

The Surroyals

Fourteen

Pavel was the first to sight the camp of Caesar's friends.
It was a clear day, and Caesar had told the sparrows
that they were near. He'd found what he said were his
friends' tracks—not footprints, but two shallow creases
running parallel to one another in the snow.

Caesar had followed them to a large spruce beside
a frozen creek when Pavel called down from the top.
"There," he said. "I think I see something."

Caesar stepped up the banks, and from his antlers
Bette could see, too. There in a clearing not far from
the creek was a shelter made of sticks and thick blan-

kets, half buried in snow, with a light plume of smoke rising from its peak.

"Is that them?" asked Rhone.

"I think so." Caesar approached slowly, but the children could not contain themselves. They flew off. "Piorello!" called Rhone, and Pavel circled the shelter two times around. "Piorello! Piorello!"

A moment passed, then suddenly one of the flaps flipped open, and out poked the face of a man.

It was a very strange face, with craggy skin and sharper features than Bette had ever seen, but kind. "Caesar!" He smiled, and stepped out to reveal a costume just as colorful and strange: he was wearing a bright red cap with earflaps, and a blue coat with red-and-yellow trim. He had a tasseled belt, and boots with upturned toes and tufts of dried grass spiking out the top.

He was happy to see his friend, Bette could tell, but as he walked up to greet them, she could also see in the hollow of his cheek and his bowlegged limp what a trying winter it had already been.

"Caesar." He took something from his coat and held it out—a mushroom. As Caesar ate from his hand, the man squinted up at the children, who'd both taken their places on the antlers again.

"Piorello?" asked Rhone.

"Pi-o-rell-o," the man replied haltingly. He took a

moment to admire the nest, then noticed the broken tine. *"Tsk, tsk."* A look of concern crossed his worn face. He examined Caesar's coat and legs, lifting up his hooves. He spoke to Caesar in calm and friendly tones, checked the sled, and finally unhitched the good strap. Then he took Caesar's reins and walked them to the foot of the shelter. "Ole, Ole," he called inside, lifting the flap. Caesar leaned his head, his antlers, and the three birds through.

The air inside was thick with smoke, but at the center Bette could make out a small birch fire, and a second man lying beside it, beneath a cover like Caesar's coat. Ole.

His eyes were bleary, and his skin was the color of birch bark, but he gave a smile much like his brother's when he saw. "Caesar." His legs kicked lightly. "Caesar." He laid his head back down.

Gaino sprinkled a handful of seeds on his brother's chest. He patted the cover for them to come, but neither Pavel nor Rhone saw. They were looking around the room, peering through the smoke for some sign of their father.

"Piorello?" called Pavel. "Piorello?"

No answer. The sick man, Ole, said something to his brother. They both gave nods, then Gaino crossed back to the door flap again, giving Caesar a kind tug on the neck as he stepped out.

Pavel looked up at Bette. "I don't think he's here, Mother."

No, she shook her head. She didn't know what more to say.

Ole spoke again. He was calling to them, gesturing weakly with his hand.

"You should eat," said Bette.

They both fluttered down to Ole's cover, but Bette could tell they weren't hungry. Rhone looked around. "Piorello," she called. "Piorello?"

"Piorello," Ole replied.

"Piorello." Gaino staggered back in, his arms now full of bundles from the sled. He carried them over to his brother's side and sat down cross-legged. He set the gifts out around them both and clapped his hands. For a moment, the two of them just looked at all they'd been brought, then Gaino began.

He chose one of the smaller bundles first. He gave it a sniff and looked up at Caesar. "Oh, good, Caesar."

He slipped a thin white bone from his boot and cut the sinews binding the bundle. The cover opened. Inside was what looked like a clump of minced brown leaves. Gaino took a smooth hollow stick from his coat and stuffed one end with a pinch. "Good, Caesar." He lit the end by a tinder from the fire. "Good." The smoke drifted from his mouth.

He offered the hollow stick to Ole, but Ole refused, so Gaino turned to the next bundle. This one was slightly larger, filled inside with what looked like shiny black pebbles. *"Mmmmmmmm."* Gaino clapped his hands again. He took a covered black pail and hung it on a stick above the fire, murmuring to his brother.

Ole nodded faintly.

Gaino opened the third and fourth bundles together. Both were filled with dried sedge grass. *"Aaaah."* He lifted out two handfuls and showed his brother. He stuffed them inside a worn pair of boots.

His brother smiled through slim, glassy eyes.

Gaino turned back to the black pebbles. He dropped a handful into a birch bowl and began grinding them down with a stone. He had to remove his mittens to work, and Bette could see how his hands were shaking, and how slender his wrists and fingers were. A lonely, trying winter.

Steam was rising from the pail now. Gaino scooped the black mulch from the bowl into another, smaller cup, and poured in the hot water. A warm aroma filled the smoky air.

Gaino offered the brew to his brother first. With frail and trembling hands, he held it to Ole's lips, but Ole's eyes were closed. Gaino palmed his brother's forehead. He whispered something soft.

There were just two bundles left—the smallest and the largest, one atop the other. He took the first, a little pouch, tied at the top with gut. Gaino slipped the knot and peeked inside. He smiled. A treat, it must have been. He set it aside for later, then turned to the last of Caesar's gifts, the one which had ridden the back seat the whole way.

Gaino sliced the gutstrings binding it. They flipped back, the bearskin cover relaxed, and with great care Gaino removed what was inside.

"Oooooh," he whispered. "Good, Caesar."

It was a drum, oval-shaped, with a long wooden handle and pale brown skin stretched across the top, etched with little black markings.

Gaino's face changed as he looked at them. It grew more sad and peaceful, and a stillness fell inside the tent. Gaino rubbed his thumb across the smooth skin of the drum. He smoked the leaves that Caesar had brought, and drank his brew, all while his brother fell deeper and deeper and deeper asleep.

Finally, Gaino pushed himself up again. He crossed to Bette and Caesar, who was still standing with just his head and neck inside. Gaino asked Caesar something. Caesar gave a faint nod and Bette fluttered down next to the fire as the two of them stepped out.

There were just the birds and Ole, the sleeping brother, now.

"Mother?" Rhone had been waiting the whole

while to speak. "Do you think we're ever going to find him?"

Through the opening in the flap, Bette could see Gaino scatter something across the snow for Caesar—hay or moss.

"I don't know."

Pavel looked up at her. "But we're going to keep looking?"

Ole's chest rose beneath them ever so faintly, then fell again, as a trail of three snowflakes drifted through the opening above.

"I don't know."

Gaino stepped back in. He sat down beside his brother and felt his forehead. "*Tk, tk,*" he clucked with his tongue, then looked at the chicks with a weary smile.

He slid the drum between his legs. From underneath, he removed a long, curved staff—an antler carved up and down with markings. Gaino took it in his hand and very gently began to tap the drum.

Tha-dump da-dum, tha-dump da-dum.

The snowflakes drifted down into the fire, and Gaino beat his antler on the drum.

Tha-dump da-dum, tha-dump da-dum.

The night outside descended. Soon the fire was their only light, and their shadows flickered on the walls of the tent, dancing to the rhythm of the drum.

Tha-dump da-dum.

The children nestled down. The constant rhythm seemed to weigh upon their eyes, heavier and heavier, and Bette was on the point of sleep herself, when through the smoke she saw something which awakened her, it was so unlike anything she'd ever seen before.

Fifteen

Bette saw the shadow of the sick brother, Ole, rise. Pavel and Rhone were sound asleep and Gaino's eyes were on the drum, tha-dump da-dum. But Ole's shadow stood up from his body and began to dance around them, round and round the flickering walls.

Finally it stopped beside his brother. The smallest of Caesar's gifts was still on Gaino's lap, still inside its pouch. Ole's shadow leaned down and took it. Gaino just kept drumming. He did not see, even as his brother's shadow turned and left, passing through the deerskin wall as though it were a mist.

Bette went after him. She followed the smoke out through the peak and looked down from the cross-sticks.

Ole's shadow was passing by Caesar now, who was standing asleep. It walked up to the sled, where two ravens perched on the tips of the runners, waiting. Now they both hopped up to Ole's shoulders, opened their wings, and lifted him into the air. But Ole's shadow did not seem to mind, even as the two dark birds flew him off into the woods.

Bette followed, keeping her silence through all the barren stalks and limbs until they came to the lip of a small hollow. The ravens dropped Ole's shadow at the edge and flew down ahead of him. Bette called. Ole looked back and saw her coming. He raised his arm, she flew to his wrist, and they both looked down together.

The ravens were at the bottom of the hollow, perched beside each other on the rock overhang which marked the entrance of a small cave. Bette recognized it—the cave where the bear made his den. It was all covered in snow, but the stake was still out front, only now its tip was a burning flame, and there was a track-beaten path leading in.

Just then, another raven appeared on the opposite side of the hollow. It glided down in a wide sweeping arc and landed beside its cousins with a brief flutter. Then behind it came a small brown rabbit with a strand of berries in its mouth. Bette and Ole watched as it hopped down the far slope and into the cave, beneath the indifferent eyes of the three stooped birds.

Ole started down as well now, with Bette still on his shoulder. The ravens clucked and cawed at their approach, but Ole only smiled back at them as he and Bette entered below.

Along the wall inside, a row of burning stakes lit a narrow

turning passageway. The rabbit was out in front of them, but Bette couldn't see where they were headed till they came round the first wide bend.

Down at the end of the passage sat a great brown bear, enthroned on a low ledge beside a much darker, unlit tunnel. He held a linden staff in his lap, and surrounding him were gifts—berries, feathers, nuts and leaves, pinecones, polished stones, and antlers.

The rabbit was bowed before him now. It lay the berries at his feet. The bear gave a nod, and the rabbit hopped off into the unlit passage, gone.

The bear swept the berries to the side with his staff. Now was Ole's turn. With Bette still on his shoulder, he crawled before the bear. He took the pouch from his belt—the one he'd lifted from his brother's lap—and opened it. Out tumbled a wedge of honeycomb.

The bear seemed pleased, but as Ole turned for the shadow, the king stopped him. "You may go," he said to Ole. "But you—" He looked at Bette. "No."

She hopped down from Ole's back. Ole gave her a nod farewell, and then crawled into the black himself. A moment and he was gone, too.

The bear turned to Bette again. "It is not your time," he said.

"Your Majesty?"

His ear turned. He recognized her voice. "You were here before," he said. "The night of the first blizzard. You stood at the entrance, whispering."

"Yes, Your Majesty. I'm sorry. We didn't mean to disturb you."

The bear shook his head. "Who is Piorello?"

She paused. She hadn't expected. "Piorello is my mate, the father of my young."

"You lost him?"

"Yes."

"And did you ever find him?"

"No."

The bear nodded. "And is that why you're here now?"

"Your Majesty?"

"To call for him." He motioned to the unlit passage.

Bette hadn't even considered. She looked into the shadow, all black and hollow. "Would he hear me?"

"If he's there."

She listened. She could hear the shadow's heart now, beating—tha-dump da-dum, tha-dump da-dum.

"Could he come back with me?" she asked.

The bear shook his head. "That is the last you'd see him."

Bette understood. It was the thought she'd been guarding against all along, what she most feared. That Piorello was gone—was here. Would never be found outside.

She stepped up to the shadow, her heart athrum. She closed her eyes and tried calling his name. "Pio—" But her voice was swallowed in fear.

"That's all right," said the bear. "Try again."

Bette faced the entrance square this time, lifted her head, and called out. "Piorello? . . . Piorello? . . . Are you there?"

Her voice echoed deep inside the cave. She waited for an an-

148

swer, hoping for silence, but there was just the drum. Tha-dump da-dum.

"Piorello? . . . Can you hear me? . . . Piorello?"

Again she listened, but once again all she heard was her song fading, and the silence drumming—tha-dump da-dum, tha-dump da-dum.

"I don't hear him," she whispered.

The bear shook his head, no.

Bette's heart lifted. He was not here, not yet. But then she thought of the forest outside, so deep and wide, and how far they'd already come, and all she could think was, where?

The bear's head tilted.

"What?" she asked.

"Something." He leaned toward the shadow.

But no, thought Bette. Not Piorello. Please, I will find him. I will keep trying. She turned her ear to the blackness. She heard the drum, tha-dump da-dum, *but there was something else, the bear was right. Something deep inside the silent thump and hiss.*

But it wasn't Piorello. It was a honking, wheezing, strumming sound. A baying.

Geese.

A flock of geese was flying over—calling down together, "Follow, follow."

She looked up to see, and there they were, at least two dozen of them, flying in formation through the pitch black of the shadow. "Follow, follow," they all called.

Then, just as they were passing over, something dropped from the beak of the lead goose—something small and white came falling down, twirling down through the black, round and round like a feather and now landing right in front of Bette, settling there at the shadow's edge:

A garland of white flowers.

The girl.

Piorello was with the girl.

Sixteen

The sound of the drumming stopped and Bette awakened to the smoky air of Ole and Gaino's home. The fire was dead. A white morning light was coming down through the smoke hole. Gaino sat with his eyes open and glazed. Pavel and Rhone were nestled on Ole's blanket, but Ole's chest lay still beneath them, and his face was a shade more pale than it had been the night before.

Bette could hear Caesar outside, digging in the snow. She flew up through the opening at the top of the shelter.

"Caesar."

He was standing at the crest of the creek bank, feeding. She flew down in front of him. "Caesar, I need to go back."

He looked at her. "Back?"

"To the willow, to the place we first took nest."

Caesar shook his head; he didn't understand.

"I had a dream," she said. "I spoke to the bear, in the cave, and I need to go back. I believe Piorello is there."

Caesar did not question. "Do you remember the way?"

"I think so." Bette looked through the woods. "It starts along the creek, I know. We follow the banks to the large spruce, and then . . ." She stopped. So much of the time, she'd been inside the nest. She hadn't seen. "Well, I suppose we can follow your tracks."

Caesar shook his head. "Not if it snows." He glanced back at his friends' meager dwelling, and at just that moment, the flap opened. Pavel and Rhone came flying out, frightened. They dashed straight to Caesar's antlers. Then came Gaino.

It hardly seemed the same man, he looked so grim. He walked toward them silently, his eyes on the snow. When he reached them, he offered no greeting. He just picked up a lump of moss, took Caesar's bridle, and started walking them back along the frozen creek, away from the shelter.

"Where are we going?" Rhone whispered.

Bette shook her head, she didn't know.

They stopped at the great spruce. Gaino slipped the bridle from Caesar's head and neck. He murmured something beneath his breath, then dropped the moss on the snow and started back.

Caesar seemed uncertain. He took a step to follow, but Gaino turned and shook his head. "No," he said more firmly now. He swept his boot over Caesar's tracks and waved him off with another brief command. Again he started back, but Caesar still did not understand. He took another step to follow, but this time when Gaino spun round, his eyes were fiery. "No!" He slapped Caesar with the reins, and the birds flurried up to a branch. He barked at Caesar and lashed again, but Caesar did not flinch or fight. He only stepped back, startled, and for a moment the two old friends stood looking at each other. Finally Gaino lowered his head. He spoke something soft and low, then for a third time started back.

Caesar kept his place. He watched Gaino limp along the banks of the creek, small and frail.

The birds flew down. "What do you think happened?" asked Rhone. "Why was he so angry?"

153

Caesar only shook his head. He did not speak until Gaino had made it all the way back, safe inside the shelter. "Was Ole in the dream you had last night?"

"Yes," said Bette.

"Will he be waking up this morning?"

Bette thought back, and remembered Ole disappearing in the shadow. "I'm sorry, Caesar."

Pavel and Rhone were too anxious to hear, or understand. Pavel looked up. "But where are we going now, Mother?"

"Home," she said quickly. "Back to the place you both were born."

"What for?" asked Rhone.

"I think your father may be there."

"Why?"

Bette looked down at her. She could understand their apprehension. They'd been through so much, waited so long, for so little.

"I just believe he is."

"Is Caesar coming?" asked Pavel.

"I don't know."

They all looked down. Caesar's gaze was still set in the distance, on the faint wisp of smoke now rising from his friends' shelter. Then, *tha-dump da-dum, tha-dump da-dum,* the thump of Gaino's drum started up again.

Caesar nodded. "I suppose."

Bette hopped down to his brow tine. She wanted to thank him, but his eyes looked so grave. She'd never seen them like that. "Caesar?" she whispered, but he didn't even seem to hear. He just turned his head and started.

Pavel and Rhone looked down, timid and silent— they could see it too, the difference—but Caesar said nothing. He pointed his antlers ahead and carried them back through the birches again, for the first time since they'd known him, free of Gaino's sled.

Seventeen

Piorello was out above the sea, and it was night. The moon was round and large, and the crest of every wave below was catching its light.

There was no land, either ahead or behind, but Piorello was not lost or tired. He was flying in a raven's wake. He could see its black wings rise and fall in front of him, obscuring the stars with each stroke. He could hear them caress the wind. And he could feel the quiet air pulling him forward.

Overhead, a heron passed, and then a falcon—and they were trailing ravens, too. The sky was filled with birds, birds of every kind, all crossing the sea behind a night-wide flock of ravens, who pierced the wind like shadows.

The raven would see him across, thought Piorello. All he had to do was stay within the raven's wake, and the winds would not harm him, not throttle him or cast him on the sea. He would see the other side.

He repeated this to himself, over and over. Just stay, be calm, safe behind the raven.

But then there was a sound—a murmur in the distance, which stilled his wings. A voice, it sounded like, but where was it coming from?

He looked up at the moon, and there it was again.

"Piorello?"

Bette.

"Are you there? . . ."

He wanted to answer, Yes, Bette, here! But he didn't dare pause. If he lost the raven, he would never get across. He'd be lost.

Yet there was her voice again.

"Piorello? . . . Can you hear me?"

This time he could not help himself. He opened his beak to call her name, the raven gave a strum, and before his voice would come, the wind swept over him. The great sky swallowed him, and just as he had feared, just as he had dreamt, he was out alone above the sea.

But the winds did not throw or throttle him, for there was her voice again.

157

"Piorello."

Calling so sweet, it seemed the night sky calmed itself to hear. Its breezes swept beneath him. He had only to turn up his wings and they carried him down in wide and winding circles, round and round toward the stirring sea below. He glided down to the waves, and when he reached the surface, the breezes cast him gently, not on the roiling surf or foam, but on the soft flat bed of an abandoned halcyon's nest.

The sea was calm. Overhead, all the other birds flew on to death, but Piorello lay in his nest; to float, to wait, a willing captive of the tide.

Bette was calling. Still.

Eighteen

The season's first snowstorm had fairly well holed the school in. The girls, with their bags all packed and ready, had had to stay over, huddled in their rooms like squirrels and sparrows. It snowed on and off for a day, but the following morning, the sun appeared again.

Bernard, the Saint Bernard, took instant advantage. A walk out to the fields might hit the spot, after so much lying about by the fire. He expected Piorello might want to come along, so before heading off, he ambled over to his friend's window, which was open its usual crack. He barked up several times, but there was no answer. Strange, he thought, but very well, too bad for Piorello—and Bernard started for the fields alone.

The snow was deep, but he'd made it most of the way across the first meadow when he caught sight of the odd stone garden by the bridge, right there where the geese had liked to rest. In the very same place, he thought. Oh, no. No, it couldn't be. He started over. Couldn't be, he thought, but then he saw it was, a whole flock of them, frozen in the snow.

He galloped over to see if he hadn't come too late. But he could smell it as he walked among the cold gray bodies. Even in the cold he could tell—much death here.

Then his nose caught the scent of something else, something still warm over by one of the goslings. He pawed at the feathers—something familiar. He brushed away the snow, and there, snuggled against the little goose's wing, he found the trembling sparrow.

"Piorello?" Bernard nudged him with his nose. "Piorello, wake up. What are you doing here?" Bernard licked him. "Piorello?" The little bird did not stir, but Bernard could taste that he was still alive. Gently he picked him up in his mouth and started back across the snow-covered fields as fast as he could. He raced all the way to the dormitory, through the flap-door to Sister Poole's room.

The sister was sitting at her desk. She gave Bernard a scolding look at first, for tracking so much snow in, but then she noticed there was something in his mouth.

She clamped his ears, and Bernard dropped the sparrow into her lap.

The sister took the bird in both her hands. She held it to her ear and rubbed its breast with her thumbs, then set him by the fire and crossed herself. With that, Bernard left again, to go find the groundsman and lead him out to the bridge.

.   .   .

Piorello awakened to the sight of a simmering fire. He was on a soft bed, on the hearth of a simple room, larger than the girl's, but with the same plain furniture.

Where am I? he thought.

He looked out the window. Snow. He remembered the geese.

But what place is this?

" 'Lo," he croaked.

At that moment, the door opened and in came the broad-chinned sister. She came straight to the hearth and picked him up. She spoke kindly to him. She offered him a small saucer of water, but he could manage only three sips before she grabbed the blanket from her chair and wrapped him warm inside. She clutched him to her chest, and hurried from the room, through two doors, then up a flight of stairs.

The girls were coming down in their coats and hats, trailed by older men in black, tilting their heads and tipping their caps. The sister rushed past them in a flurry, up another flight of stairs and down a long hallway.

Midway, she stopped and rapped on a door. She opened it and Piorello could see it was the girl's room. There was his shroud and his dishes, and the window was open a crack, but the girl was not there. Her bed was made, but the dolls were gone.

The sister crossed to shut the window, then hurried out again. Still clutching Piorello to her chest, she bustled down the hall, down the stairs, and straight out to her bicycle. She set Piorello snug in the basket and started through the gates, pedaling madly.

Between the wicker weave Piorello could see the lane descending from the hillcrest. There was a train of horse-drawn carriages all lined in a row, with great banks of snow piled up on both sides.

The sister took the slope without braking, ringing a little bell as she descended. "Make way! Make way!" she called. The girls looked out from their windows as she raced by.

. . .

Elsbeth was no longer crying when she heard her name being called from behind.

"Miss Bonner! Miss Bonner!"

It sounded like Sister Poole's voice.

Elsbeth looked out the window of the carriage, and there she was on her bicycle, her great black cape billowing behind her. "Mr. Doogan. Stop the coach."

"Miss Bonner." The sister slowed to a stop at her window.

"Sister, is something wrong?" Elsbeth was embarrassed. She could feel her face was still red and damp.

The sister took a moment to catch her breath, then reached down for the blanket in her basket. "I found a friend of yours, Miss Bonner." She opened the blanket and showed her. "He was calling for you."

The bird. Elsbeth couldn't believe her eyes.

"He's had a difficult few days," the sister cautioned, "but I think that with some care, he'll be fine."

"Oh, yes. Thank you, Sister." The girl reached out and took him in her hands.

"You can have the blanket, too. Keep him warm."

"Yes, Sister. Thank you!"

"My pleasure, child." She leaned over to look at the bird. "And you be well, little one. Merry Christmas, Miss Bonner."

"Merry Christmas, Sister! And thank you." She couldn't possibly have said how much.

The sister gave Mr. Doogan a wave to continue on, then turned and started back up the road on her bicycle, pedaling more temperately now, and offering stately nods to the girls as their hands appeared from out the windows to wave.

Mr. Doogan turned round. "You have everything, Miss Elsbeth?"

"I do, Mr. Doogan. Thank you."

She pulled her head back inside the carriage and looked down at the bird, her heart still thumping with thanks and relief, and wonder at his return. "But where have you been?" she whispered. "I was so worried."

The bird was nearly too weary to answer. Just the faintest, most plaintive call, then he laid down his head to rest against her palm.

And yet, it was strange—for the first time, she thought she understood. All he wanted was to go home again. That's all he'd ever wanted.

She leaned her head out the window. "Mr. Doogan."

"Miss Elsbeth?"

"You understand, I am to go to Newcastle, not London."

He stopped the carriage and looked back. "Ma'am?"

"That's what Miss Poole said. She said she just received word from Father, a telegram from the continent. We're to spend Christmas with my grandmother."

Mr. Doogan's brow slanted. He hadn't heard any such thing. "Does Master Miles know?"

"I assume," said Elsbeth. "I assume he's on his way already."

Mr. Doogan looked back at her a moment, confused and leery. "She's all right, your grandmother?"

"I don't know," Elsbeth replied. "I hope. All I know is we're supposed to go . . . Please, Mr. Doogan. We have to."

She looked at him, and it was the plea in her eye that seemed to do the trick.

He nodded faintly. "As you wish." He turned and gave the reins a gentle snap. "All right, Winnie, you heard Miss Elsbeth."

"Thank you, Mr. Doogan!"

And so it was—as the good Sister Poole witnessed when she finally reached the top of the hill again—while all the other carriages turned left at Foxridge Road and headed for Darlington station, Elsbeth Bonner's turned right, where lay nothing of note but the Newcastle wharf and the daily steamer.

PART VI

The Return

Nineteen

Caesar followed a different route back, and his pace was quicker than before, now that there wasn't the sled tugging at him from behind. Bette wasn't entirely sure where they were, but thought better than to ask. Caesar didn't seem to be in much of a mood for talking.

He was unusually quiet, in fact, and his silence had the effect of quieting Pavel and Rhone as well. They spent most of their time on his antlers, leaving only every now and then to look for food. They did not sing or speak much. What conversations they had, they reserved for their flights among the brittle trees, and these all concerned Caesar's mood. "Is something wrong with him?" they'd ask. "Is he angry with us?"

"No" was always Bette's reply. "He just wants to get us there, and I suspect he's concerned about his friend."

Finally, the third day out, Caesar stopped beside a thicket of brambles and spoke his first words since leaving Gaino. "Eat," he said. "And gather, as much as you can find."

Bette was taken by surprise. She hopped up to the branch of a nearby birch, just to gauge her prospects, and over the bramble she saw a vast expanse of white.

"Caesar, is that the lake?"

Pavel and Rhone fluttered up to see.

"Yes."

"And where is the willow?" asked Rhone. "Which way?"

"Straight," said Caesar.

The three birds peered through the trees for some sign of the far side, but there wasn't any—not even a horizon line—with the sky so white.

"But there's no end," said Pavel.

"There is," said Caesar. "You just can't see it."

"How many days will it take us from here?" asked Bette.

"Three. Maybe four."

"Four?" She looked down. She'd been thinking many more. "Around?"

Caesar shook his head. "Across."

Pavel and Rhone looked at one another excitedly, but Bette felt nothing but worry.

"Pavel, Rhone," she spoke with conspicuous calm, "would you excuse us a moment? Why don't you go see if you can find some food."

As Pavel and Rhone flew off, Bette descended once again to Caesar's antlers. "Caesar, did you say across?"

He nodded. "Four days and we'll be there."

"But the cold."

"We should be thankful for the cold. The ice will bear us."

Bette looked back through the bramble. "And how long would it take going around?"

"Another moon. Too long. We'll be fine, just as long as you bring enough to eat. You can keep it in the nest."

"And what about you?"

"I'll be all right. Now go." He began hoofing the snow for heather.

Bette looked down at him. He was being awfully stubborn, she wasn't sure why, but it didn't seem he was leaving any choice.

She called. "Pavel? Rhone?"

A frozen lingonberry bush answered in two voices. "Yes, Mother?"

Bette flew over and in. "Pavel, don't eat now. We've a long journey ahead."

"Then we are crossing?" asked Rhone.

"Yes. But we'll need to save what we find, and keep it in the nest."

"But there really isn't anything." Pavel shook his head frankly.

Bette took a glance about the bush and saw it was true. The dead of winter was no time to be looking for food in an unfamiliar part of the forest.

Then she caught sight of something outside, up near the long branch of an alder. An old squirrel was peeking down at them.

"Hello," she called. The squirrel ducked quickly inside his hole, but she started up anyway. Pavel and Rhone followed.

"Hello?" They landed next to the hole. "Excuse me?"

The hole was silent.

"Hello—"

"Some of us are trying to sleep," came an annoyed voice.

"I know," she whispered. "I'm sorry to disturb you, but I couldn't help seeing you were out, and my young and I are in need of some help."

Another moment passed.

"Hello—"

"What kind of help?"

"We're making a journey—"

"We're crossing the lake!" Pavel leaned around.

"Yes," said Bette, "so we need to gather food. I know it's a great deal to ask, but I was wondering if you could spare us any part of your store—"

"Share a part of my—" The hole sputtered, then suddenly the squirrel popped his head out. "What is the meaning of this? You can't ask for part of my store. You should have taken stock yourself."

"I know, but we haven't had any time."

"What have you been doing?"

"Traveling."

"Well, this is no time to travel. It's the middle of winter."

"I know," said Bette again, "but we have to get to the other side of the lake."

"The other side of the—" The squirrel sputtered again. "For what possible reason?"

"Our father's there," said Rhone.

"We hope," reminded Bette.

"You hope? Well, you better do more than hope if you intend to cross the lake." He looked at Bette reproachfully. "Couldn't you at least take your young around?"

It was a good question. That would have been Bette's preference, too.

"But we have to get there soon," said Pavel.

"And we're not going alone," added Rhone. "Tell him, Mother. Caesar is taking us." She nodded over toward the bramble, where Caesar had found some moss beneath the snow.

The squirrel looked down. His whiskers twitched. He still did not approve. "I'm sorry. It's the middle of winter."

Bette didn't insist. She understood. "Maybe if you could tell us where there's a good bush, or a pine tree."

The squirrel only shook his head. "But everything's taken, don't you understand?" He ducked back down inside the hole, and Bette could hear him scamper down to his winter bed.

He was right, though. She looked up at the cold, bleak forest again. She didn't know where she'd ever find enough.

Then—*tick–tock–click–snap*—something came tripping down the branches from above and landed with a thump in the snow.

Pavel flew down to see. "It's an acorn."

"But this isn't an acorn tree." Rhone looked up curiously. "Where do you think it came from?"

Bette wasn't sure.

Then across the way came the sound of something else falling down from the treetops.

Pavel went to inspect this one, too. "Seeds."

"Mother, look." Rhone pointed down to the roots of the neighboring fir. A little pair of paws was pushing out a strand of lingonberries.

"Good luck," came two timid voices. Rabbits.

Bette was taken aback. "Thank you."

Then all of a sudden, like the remnants of an afternoon shower, more nuts and seeds began to trickle down from the canopy, dropped from all the little winter doors, ticking and tocking and thumping down into the snow.

Pavel swept up the strand of lingonberries first, and flew them back to Caesar's antlers.

"Thank you," called Bette. She sang it out to all the stolid trees, then she and Rhone did the same as Pavel, and began gathering the rest.

Before long the pile inside the nest was so large, the bottom began to sag.

"I don't think we can take much more," said Bette finally. "Caesar, is it too heavy?"

As he shook his head, the nest shifted sluggishly.

"Yes, that's enough. Pavel? Rhone?"

The birds took their places on the antlers. The nest shifted back again, and Caesar walked them to the nearest opening along the bank.

"Thank you, all," Bette called one last time.

"Thank you," echoed Rhone.

Then Caesar stepped down onto the endless stretch of white.

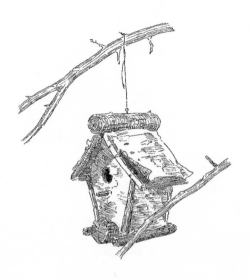

Twenty

From the very first turn of their coach, Piorello could tell the girl was taking him back. It was nothing about the direction they'd chosen—all he could feel was the carriage swinging him back and forth—but as he lay in her lap, adrift between waking and sleep, he could tell in the way she touched him, the way she covered her smiling mouth as she looked out the window. The only other time he'd seen her so happy was on the bird-walk at home, holding out seeds for the flock.

The trip took five days, and the man who drove the carriage accompanied them the whole way. First, he brought them to a large boat that puffed smoke from a large black stack, just like the one they'd taken on the way over. It was a three-day crossing. Then they climbed aboard a giant carriage, like a great long snake, but with a terrible growl. Over the mountains and down again they came to a second boat with a pine tree at the top, and from there it was another day's trip, which the Seed Girl and Piorello spent almost entirely out in the open air, happy to brave the cold because they knew, they both could feel, every passing moment was bringing them closer.

The last leg of the journey they rode by carriage again. A great woolly plow horse pulled them from the pier through a village and into a snowy countryside. Piorello was feeling much better now, but with the carriage rocking them back and forth, the sky a luminous blue half-light, and the distant mountains with their heads all buried in the clouds, he was sound asleep when they finally arrived.

The girl woke him gently, lifting him out of her pocket. They'd stopped before a grand house with a snow-covered roof, and a birch forest on both sides. Piorello could see the lakefront through the windows, and the lake. They were here. They were home.

It was strange, though. As the girl took Piorello up the path to the front steps, he looked out at the woods. After all this time away, all the days and nights waiting for this very moment, he'd have thought he'd want to fly straight out now. Go find Bette as soon as he could. But as he looked out from the Seed Girl's pocket, over at all the sleeping trees, so bare and quiet, so unlike the trees he'd left last summer, he felt strangely timid. For the first time it occurred to him, Bette might not even be in the willow anymore, not with the cold. She'd probably moved.

Before he could even begin to think where, they were ascending the front steps, and the door of the home was swinging open.

.   .   .

"Elsbeth?" Miss Gulbrandsen was standing in front of them, an expression of utter dismay on her face. "What are you doing here, child?"

Elsbeth didn't answer at first. Mr. Doogan set down the bags and removed his hat. "Mr. Bonner isn't here?"

"Mr. Bonner?" Miss Gulbrandsen looked back at Elsbeth again. "Was your father supposed to be here?"

Elsbeth shrugged. "I thought so" was all she could say. "Is Gramma in?"

Miss Gulbrandsen was doing her best to appear cross. "Of course." She stepped aside. "Here." She handed Elsbeth a tea tray from the foyer table. "She's in the parlor."

Elsbeth went straight in, with the tray in her hands and the bird in her pocket. Mr. Doogan started upstairs with the bags, and Miss Gulbrandsen followed, still shaking her head.

Gramma was sitting in a wing chair by the fire, resting her eyes. Elsbeth entered as quietly as she was able and poured her a cup of steaming hot tea.

The vapors seemed to rouse her, but her eyes remained closed. "Elsbeth?"

"Yes."

"That was quick." She reached out her hand. Elsbeth took it and sat down on the bricks.

"You sound as if you were expecting me."

Gramma smiled, eyes still closed. "I suspect Tibel must have whispered something in my ear."

"Has he been acting up?"

"Oh, terrible." She shook her head ruefully. "Leaving doors and windows open. Miss Gulbrandsen thinks he's up to something out in the woods." She opened her eyes to give a wink.

"I missed you, Gramma. I thought of you every day."

"And I you." She squeezed her hand, then noticed the bird. "I see you've brought a friend."

"Brought him back." Elsbeth held him up. "He's from the woods. He was hurt, but now he's better, see?"

"Looks as if he's been lonely."

"Yes."

Just then there came a whistle from outside, of someone calling to the wood. Elsbeth sat up. "Is that Uncle Per?"

"Mm-hm."

"He's here?"

"He came this morning. I think that's him putting the sheaves out."

"Can I go see?"

"If you button your coat."

"Thank you, Gramma." Elsbeth hugged her, and kissed her on both cheeks. "I'm happy."

"I'm happy, too."

Elsbeth took her bird and started for the stairs.

. . .

Piorello had heard the call as well, a strange song coming from somewhere high and remote. But such a confusing place this was—all twists and turns and doors and hallways. The girl carried him up two flights, and then a third, more narrow staircase. They came into a long, dark room with an angled ceiling and an open window at one end.

The call was coming from just outside. The girl ran across and leaned her head out.

From her pocket, Piorello could see there was a young man with hay-colored hair standing on the roof. The snow had been cleared from the shingles, and there was a large bundle of grain hanging from the brick chimney.

The man cried out happily when he saw the girl, and offered his arm to welcome her out, just as the first birds came flying in from the birches—a family of blackbirds—and now two squirrels scampering over the gutter.

Maybe Bette would come, too, thought Piorello, or Pavel or Rhone. He hopped from her pocket and looked out hopefully. Why, even now the first sparrows were flying in and landing.

"Emil!" he called out to the first. It was Bette's cousin.

"Piorello?" Emil took a hop over when he saw. "Is that you?"

"Where's Bette?"

"Bette?" Emil seemed confused. "We thought she was with you."

"She's not in the wood?"

"No," said Emil.

"Piorello?" Piorello's cousin Greta landed beside Emil; they were mates, it was clear. Their young were just now landing behind them, three smaller sparrows. "Piorello, what are you doing here? Where's Bette?"

"I don't know," he said. He looked to Emil for some explanation.

Emil did his best. "She did wait for you. She called and called, and we all looked, but then one morning she stopped. We went to see, and she was gone, too."

"With Pavel and Rhone?"

Emil nodded. "That was a long time ago, Piorello. There were leaves."

Piorello was stunned. He didn't know what to say.

"Mother? Father?" The young sparrows were calling over from the sheaf. "Aren't you coming?"

Emil looked at Greta awkwardly. "We should probably go tell the others, about the grain."

"Do you want to come?" Greta turned to Piorello. "I'm sure they'll be happy to see you."

Piorello was still speechless. Over by the chimney, the Seed Girl laughed. She and the man were standing arm in arm, feeding a young sparrow from their hands.

"Piorello?" Greta was waiting for his answer.

But he didn't want to see the others now, not like this. "I think I'll wait."

"All right." Emil took a hop back. "But we'll tell them we saw you. And, Piorello, welcome back."

"Yes, welcome back," said Greta.

They both looked at him a moment, uncertain what more they could do or say, then off they flew, as a pair, back to the wood to summon the others.

The Seed Girl and the man were heading in now.

It was cold, and their coats were thin. They climbed under the sash, and Piorello went in, too. The girl shut the window, but Piorello didn't go back downstairs with them. He stayed at the window, hiding in the shadow, watching all the birds come to feed. He'd hoped that maybe Emil was wrong. Maybe Bette was just the other side of the house, and maybe she'd come, too.

But the grain didn't last very long. All the birds who stayed the winter came in to take their share, stem by stem, bud by bud. Soon it was dark, and the sheaf was bare. All the flocks had come and gone, and neither Bette nor Rhone nor Pavel had shown. Piorello had made it all the way back, and they were not here.

Twenty-one

The trip across the frozen lake started out not so badly. Caesar's mood hadn't improved. He remained silent, focused on a destination which as yet none of them could see—but his pace was quick and steady. A layer of crisp snow kept his hooves from the slippery ice, and at least while the sun was up, Pavel and Rhone hopped along beside him, darting out front and waiting for him to catch up.

Bette was worried, though. She wasn't comfortable out there, with the woods so far away. It was just a tiny hedge in the distance now, etching the difference between an icy gray above and an icy gray below.

As evening fell and the gray turned a more steely blue, Bette's worries were confirmed. With no glow upon the sky and the wind unfettered by trees, a terrible cold set in. She had to call Pavel and Rhone back to the nest. "And you, Caesar—if it gets much colder, promise me you'll head back for the woods again."

Caesar said nothing.

"Caesar? Promise."

He gave no answer. He just kept his pace and his aim, pointed straight ahead. So finally Bette climbed down inside the nest as well.

That night was long and frigid. The velvet wrapping of the nest did well to shield the sparrows, and with all of them together, huddled down in their bed of seeds, the children were even able to sleep briefly.

But Caesar was not so fortunate. Bette could hear the wind outside, howling and lashing at him, and she could feel him stagger and lean against it, every step. He never once faltered from his purpose, but the more he struggled in the freezing cold, the more upset she became—for what if she'd been wrong? What if Piorello wasn't there? She'd only had a dream.

The sun did return finally. A meek light slanted through the top of the nest, and Rhone awoke, shivering.

"Are we close?" she asked.

"I don't know," said Bette. "I don't think so."

Pavel stirred. "Caesar said three days."

"But can't we go back to the woods?" asked Rhone. "It's too cold."

Bette agreed. She lifted her head out into the whistling wind.

All was a gray-white mist, no trees ahead, or even to the side anymore. "Caesar?" She looked down and her breath caught short. His eyes were just barely open, his muzzle hanging with icicles, his coat all white.

"Oh, Caesar," she pled. "Please, tell me you'll turn."

No answer. Just the mist puffing from his mouth.

"But we needn't get there so soon. We can go round."

Caesar said nothing. He gave just the faintest shake of his head, then a nod out in front of them. Ahead was the way.

The wind snapped and Bette tumbled back inside the nest.

"Are we going back?" asked Rhone.

No, Bette shook her head. "He wants to cross."

And so they remained, trapped in their nest for two more icy days, while Caesar beat on below.

Twenty-two

Piorello wasn't quite sure what to do. His first night back he spent inside the house. The girl set up his nest just the same as across the water, with the same soft red blanket, but he couldn't sleep. Surely he hadn't come all the way back for this. To be here. Surely he should be out in the forest, looking for Bette. But where? Where could she be? He kept thinking of what Emil had said—how one day she'd been in the nest calling for him; the next, gone.

It was a long night, but as soon as the sun returned, he had the girl let him out. He went straight to the lakeside wood to find out what he could. He flew from tree to tree asking all the sparrows he could find if anybody knew anything more. He must have awakened the entire flock, but they were no more help than Emil. Bette was gone, they said. She'd taken the chicks with her. No one knew where.

Piorello wondered if he should just go then. Leave the wood and look for her on his own. He wanted to, but the question remained—where? No one could even tell him which way she'd gone, and darkness was falling again—these days were much too brief. Reluctantly, Piorello returned to the house.

The girl was waiting for him with a new dish of seeds and a bowl of fresh water. As discouraged as Piorello was, the girl seemed much happier now. She and the man from the roof played songs together in the room with the fire, but even afterwards, after they'd all retired to their separate beds, Piorello could still hear—the secrets she whispered didn't sound so desperate or wanting anymore. They sounded thankful. She at least seemed to have found what she'd been looking for.

For Piorello, though, it promised to be another restless night. Long after the light had died and the girl was sound asleep, he sat up in his nest thinking about tomorrow, what he would do. First, he'd check the willow, just to see, then he supposed he might cross to the other side of the road and explore the wood there. There was a hollow spruce he could probably reach by sundown, though what he would do for food, he didn't know.

But it was right then, just as he was plotting his course, trying to remember all the places he might find seeds or shelter, Piorello heard a soft click inside the room. He looked over at the door. Strange. The latch was rising off its hook, and now the door was slowly swinging open.

Piorello climbed from the nest and hopped over. No one was there, but there were the stairs, leading down. Piorello followed them, step by step, down one long flight and then another, until he found himself at the threshold of a room he hadn't been in yet.

It was a much colder room than the others, and darker. The only light was a dim blue haze that hovered against a set of three windows facing the lake. But there was one more window too, over in the corner, and that was the reason for the cold. It was slimmer than the others, and slanted to face the birches, but the sash was open a crack, and the night air was sweeping in.

Piorello wondered, could he just go? Now, in the middle of the night? He hopped across the rugs, and up onto the sill. The moon was full and bright. He should. He could go to the willow right now, and then be on his way. No need to wait. The sooner he left, the sooner he might find her.

Just like that, he ducked beneath the sash and flew. He swept across the smooth blue blanket, past the beech and into the birches. With the ground covered in snow, the path was just a faint parting of the trees, but he knew the way. He flew inside the sleeping forest, over the lattice of blue shadows. He turned at the juniper bush and followed toward the lake until he came to it, leaning out over the water, its frayed braids frozen in the ice.

He landed on the ledge of the bath and looked up inside. He wasn't exactly sure why he'd come or what he expected to find, but he was still startled by the sight: there, perched on the long branch that forked overhead, was a snow-white owl, looking right back down at him.

"Excuse me," said Piorello. "I didn't mean to disturb you."

The owl turned his head calmly. "No bother."

But he was standing on the very branch, the very spot where the nest had been.

"Can I help you?"

"No." Piorello was stilled by the owl's fierce brow. "No. I am just looking for someone."

"Whom?"

"Three sparrows, actually, like me."

190

The owl tilted his head. "Your name isn't Piorello, is it?"

"It is. How did you know?"

The owl nodded calmly. "Bette, the mother, was calling for you."

"You've seen Bette?"

"And the chicks. Very sweet."

"Where?"

"Well." The owl glanced down at the limb beneath his toes. "Here. But that was a while ago."

"Do you know where they went?"

The owl shook his head. "I imagine it was to look for you, though. She wanted to find you."

Piorello paused. Of course, he'd thought this, too, but the forest was so large, so quiet and deep. He looked out through the trees. "I just wish I knew where to begin."

The owl acted surprised. "To look for her, you mean?"

Piorello nodded.

"Well, I suppose you could try," the owl said dubiously. "But they might be anywhere, don't you think?"

"Yes," said Piorello. The birches did seem endless all of a sudden. "But I can't just wait."

"Well, let's think this through first." The owl seemed to take the problem on as his own. "Now, in my experience at least, whenever two birds are trying to find one another—or two rabbits, two mice, two anything—it's always best if one of them stays still, yes? Otherwise, you run the risk of one of you heading off in one direction, while the other comes back another, and wouldn't that be folly?"

Yes, nodded Piorello, that would be folly.

"So it seems the first question you have to ask yourself, before you just go flying off some random way, is whether you think she's *still* looking for you."

Piorello thought. "Well, I'd hope not. I'd hope she's found some shelter by now."

"One would hope," the owl agreed, "but what do you suspect?"

Piorello shook his head. He hadn't even considered, but now as he thought of it, he had heard Bette calling, in his dream. "Well, I suppose it's possible."

"Of course it's possible," the owl concurred. "So then the question becomes—if she *is* still looking— where would it be best for you to stay and wait. Yes?"

"I suppose." Piorello still wasn't convinced, but the owl was looking down at him, expectantly now.

"So? Any ideas?"

"Well . . . no," Piorello stammered. "I don't know. I mean, I hadn't thought."

"Well, perhaps you should," said the owl. "Let's do. You and I, we'll try together. We'll think: where should Piorello wait for Bette? Agreed?"

Piorello did not answer. He thought the owl might be making fun of him, but the owl persisted. He closed his eyes and hunched his wings. Then he began clucking his tongue and mumbling to himself—"Where, where, where?"

It all seemed too silly to Piorello. He had half a mind to leave, to be gone before the owl opened his eyes again. But at just that moment, the moon passed over. It was a full moon, and its light shone down through the braids directly on the owl's breast. Piorello couldn't help looking. Such a perfect, glowing white, it even seemed to glance back down again, like a beam cast from the moon's face, down onto the owl's breast, then down again to the foot of the tree. Piorello followed with his eye, and saw something he hadn't noticed before.

Right there beside the bath, a thin stake was jutting up from the snow, and there was a vine grown around it with a white blossom at the top—even now, in the gloom of a winter's night—a white flower just like the one from the window, like the ones from the Seed Girl's hair.

Piorello couldn't help a murmur of awe.

"Hm?" The owl awoke from his distraction and glanced down. "Oh." He seemed not surprised, but pleased. "Well, look at that."

"Has this been here long?" asked Piorello.

"Oh, I think I may have noticed it climbing the stake, but this is the first it's bloomed—if that's what you mean." He looked at Piorello with a gardener's pride. "So? Come up with any answers?"

"Well. I guess I'll stay here."

"You do?"

Piorello looked back down at the open flower. "Yes, I do. If that's all right."

"That's fine," the owl said. "In fact"—he looked up at the moon, which had passed behind the willow branches again—"I should probably be heading off myself. Good luck to you, Piorello. I think you make a wise choice."

"Yes, thank you. Thank you very much . . ." he groped for the name.

"Tibel," the owl offered.

"Thank you, Tibel."

With that, the owl opened his white wings and left the perch, ducking through the braids and gliding back into the woods, back in the direction of the house.

Piorello did not wonder. He gave one more look at the flower beaming up at him, then jumped to the forked branch and hopped down to a little cubby near the trunk, to sit and wait, just as Tibel had suggested.

Twenty-three

The fourth day out on the frozen lake broke with more promise. Bette emerged to find a milder sky, shrouded in mist. "Good morning, Caesar."

He offered nothing in return, just a huff and a puff as he trotted on.

"Were you all right last night?"

Another huff and a puff, that was all.

"Caesar, would you like some seeds? We have more than enough."

Still no answer. So stubborn, she thought.

Then out ahead, something caught her eye. There

was something in the ice. "Caesar, look." It wasn't very large, the size of a boulder jutting up from the lake, but different from a boulder—more like a shell of some kind. "What do you think it is?"

Caesar did not answer. He did not even turn. He just kept straight on his line, even as this odd shape hovered out to the left.

Bette could see now, though—it was a boat, frozen in the ice. Just its rim was peeking out above the surface of the snow, but she recognized it from the summer. The people liked to sit in these and float out on the water—the boy from the house had, and just the thought of it, the sight of it, lifted her heart.

But Caesar just kept huffing and puffing, and passing the little boat by.

Bette jumped down to his brow antler. "Caesar, there might be food inside. Don't you want to stop?" She hopped. "Stop!"

At last, he did.

Bette jumped out onto the snow in front of him, angry now. She was ready to scold him for being so obstinate, but then her breath caught short. His eyes. The right was closed, as it had been almost since they came on the lake, but the left was wide open, gaping. Frozen.

"Caesar, can you see me?"

He did not answer.

She hopped back up to his antler again and spoke into his ear. "Can you hear me?"

He nodded faintly.

"Mother?" The children were stirring in the nest. "Mother?" It was Rhone's voice. "May we come out?"

Bette hesitated. She looked down at Caesar's eye again. It looked terrible. "Caesar, you should have said something."

She'd tried to keep her voice low, but Pavel's head poked out now. "Why did we stop? Are we there?"

"Not yet," said Bette.

Rhone emerged. "Is Caesar all right?"

"He's all right," said Pavel.

They both looked down, though. Caesar was shivering, trembling beneath them, as much from exhaustion as from the cold.

"Is he, Mother?" Rhone sounded scared.

Bette didn't know what to say, but then in the distance she heard something, a faint chiming.

Rhone tilted her head. She heard it, too. "What's that sound?"

"Bells." Bette looked down. "Caesar, do you hear?"

His ear turned.

"We're almost there."

Pavel and Rhone looked at one another excitedly,

and as the distant knell kept on, Caesar started up again, slowly at first but then quicker and quicker, bound for the same point as he'd been aiming the last three days—straight ahead—where now, as the sun began to burn away the morning mist, Bette could see trees. Birch trees.

Twenty-four

Piorello was awakened in the morning by a strange thwacking sound. He hopped out from his little cubby in the willow and gave a look around. It had snowed during the night. The wood was coated in a fresh layer of white. No sign of Bette.

He checked the bath. The stake was there but the flower was gone, either buried or vanished, he didn't know. He wondered if it had ever really been there. Even the owl seemed like a distant dream now, in the pale daylight.

But—*thwack, thwack, thwack*—there was that sound

again, coming from near the house. He flew off to see.

The Seed Girl and the man from the roof were at the edge of the wood, and the man was hacking at the base of one of the small pine trees with a long heavy blade. Another two blows and the tree fell on the snow with a bustle. As the man hoisted it over his shoulder, the girl turned and saw Piorello. She called to him; she held out her hand. The man was starting back to the house, and she was inviting Piorello to come along.

Cold and hungry, he accepted. He wasn't sure if he should begin his search today, or stay and continue his vigil at the willow, but either way, it seemed like a good idea to warm himself by the fire and maybe have some seeds before returning.

The girl obliged, as usual. She brought him into the golden room, and set his dishes on the long, warm shelf above the fire, then she went to help her friend with the tree. They were trying to stand it up again. The coachman came in to lend a hand. Together they moved back all the furniture and spread out a red blanket on the floor. The two older women even came in and watched awhile. They brought food with them, and warm drinks, but as soon as the tree was up and straight, quiet descended again. Everyone left but the Seed Girl and Piorello.

He should go now, he knew, while the sun was still up. But the fire was crackling below and the girl was settling in for a nap. He gave himself one more moment. He took his last few seeds over to the window and looked out. He was trying to decide which direction he should follow, if he did start his search—whether he should go to the right or the left of the lake—but his eye kept returning to a curious speck out in the middle.

Or it seemed a speck at first, except that it was moving. Piorello peered through the waning light. It was an animal of some kind—a deer, trotting this way. What a cold and lonely sight, thought Piorello, a solitary reindeer come all the way across the frozen lake, now headed for the wood.

He watched it all the way until it passed behind the shoulder of birches, then Piorello turned back to the room. The time had come; he should go. He was going to call to the girl, for her to let him out, but just as he was about to open his beak, a boy came in the room—the boy from last summer, the one from the boat—and he was carrying a great load of bundles in his arms.

· · ·

"Miles?" Elsbeth could hardly believe her eyes. Her brother was standing next to the tree, with a stack of presents down at his feet. "Miles, what are you doing here?"

"Tracking down Little Miss Whatever-she-wants."

"Is Father here?"

"Yes. Upstairs."

"Is he angry?"

"He was." Miles let this idea sit a moment. "But no." He looked around suspiciously. "Is there a window open?" He saw the bird. "And what is that doing in here?"

"It's my friend. He came to school with me."

"What do you mean 'he came to school' with you?"

"You don't recognize him?"

"Where from?"

"From summer. The window in Tibel's room."

Miles looked over at the bird again and sneered. "Is not."

.   .   .

And it was just then, just as the Seed Girl started pulling the boy over by the arm, Piorello heard something from outside. A call. He jumped to the pane. There it was again. His name, coming from the wood.

The girl was holding out her hand to him, but he dashed away. He flew straight to the cold blue room, and heard it for the third time now—Bette's voice, coming from the tree-line.

"Piorello!"

"Bette!" The window was open. He ducked beneath the sash and flew. "Bette!"

"Piorello!"

She was perched on the feeder at the beech tree,

and when she saw him coming, she jumped up. "Piorello!" she called. "Piorello!"

He chased her around the outstretched limbs.
"Bette!" he sang. "Piorello," she answered, and his heart
nearly burst at the sound. Round and round, they
chased each other three times around the beech before finally landing on the branch above the feeder.

Piorello looked at her. She seemed smaller. Her
feathers were tired and worn, but he'd never seen a
sparrow so beautiful. "But where have you been?"

"Oh, Piorello. So far. We were all the way on the
far side of the lake looking for you."

"And Pavel and Rhone? Are they here?"

At just that moment, two young sparrows came
racing up the path, but they both stopped straight
when they saw him, another bird perched beside their
mother.

"There they are." Bette did her best to calm herself. "Pavel, Rhone, come meet your father."

They stood in the snow, stunned and bashful.

"Rhone?"

She hopped forward.

"Come up," called Bette, and the young sparrow
jumped up to the roof of the feeder.

"Hello, Father."

"Hello, Rhone."

Bette turned. "And Pavel?"

203

He sprung up beside his sister and bowed his head. "Father."

"Pavel."

The two young birds both kept their heads low. "Look at you." Piorello flew down beside them. "I see you're splendid fliers."

"Yes!" Pavel's chest puffed out. "See how!" He jumped up and circled the tree.

"That's excellent." Piorello turned to Rhone now. "And you've a lovely voice."

"We've been singing to you." She nodded.

"Do," said Pavel. "Show him."

Rhone stood square and called out his name—"*Piorello . . . Piorello . . .*"

Piorello listened. "And I heard you," he nodded. "I did."

"But where were you, Father?"

"Yes, Father, where?"

"Not here all along?" Bette looked at him, fearfully almost.

"Oh, no. No, I've been in such a faraway place— such a faraway place, I can hardly believe it's all happened." He looked down at the two young sparrows again in amazement.

"But we should tell Caesar!" said Pavel.

"Yes, Caesar!" Rhone echoed.

"Caesar?" Piorello turned to Bette. "Who is Caesar?"

Bette hesitated, then turned back toward the wood, where just now a weary reindeer came walking up the path—the reindeer from the lake.

"That is Caesar," said Bette.

The deer stopped. Piorello saw there was a nest perched on his left antler.

"Caesar," Bette said softly. "This is Piorello."

The deer tilted his head to look at him.

"Do you believe it, Caesar?" Pavel flew over to his antler. "We found Father."

The deer gave a faint nod, and for a moment he and Piorello looked at one another with a mixture of wonder and apprehension.

"But I have made a friend as well," said Piorello finally. "A girl." He turned to Pavel and Rhone. "Would you like to meet her?"

"May we, Mother?"

"Yes, Mother, may we?"

"It's perfectly safe," said Piorello. "She's back inside the house." He turned to Caesar. "Do you want to come?"

Caesar glanced in the direction of the house and shook his head.

Bette wondered, though. Caesar looked worn and

tired, barely himself, and yet there still seemed some-thing so determined about him, as if his work wasn't yet done. She turned to Piorello. "You go ahead with the children. I'll be right there."

Piorello nodded. "Be careful, though, when you come. You can't fly through to the light. You have to wait on the sill, and we'll come get you."

"I will," Bette replied, and Piorello started Pavel and Rhone across the snow.

Bette and Caesar watched the two of them follow their father up the slope and round to the lighted win-dows facing the lake. They could hear them call, the window open, then close again.

Bette turned back to her friend. "I wanted to thank you, Caesar. For everything you've done. You know, we could never . . . I don't know what we would have done if not for you."

Caesar said nothing. He was still looking at the house.

"Are you sure you don't want to come in? They're very nice, I've seen them."

Caesar shook his head. "I have to go."

"Go?"

"As soon as I find something to eat." He looked around at the woods.

Bette didn't understand. "Do you mean back to the herd?"

Caesar shook his head. "To Gaino."

But that didn't make sense, thought Bette. Gaino had banished him, had struck him. "Do you think he'll take you?"

Caesar nodded. Again, he seemed so sure, and suddenly Bette understood—the reason he'd been so determined to cross the lake. He'd known all along he was going back. He'd only wanted to see them safe, but he'd never intended leaving Gaino.

He looked so worn and tired, though.

"At least tell me you'll go around," said Bette. "You can't go back across."

Caesar shook his head. "I'll be fine. As long as I get enough to eat." He looked back at the woods again. "I'm sure there's moss somewhere."

Bette looked at him, shivering. "I know where there's some."

She led him behind the pines—there was a drift there, she remembered from the summer. Caesar nuzzled the snow and nodded. He could smell it. "Thank you." He raised his head and looked at Bette with his good eye. "You'll say goodbye to Pavel and Rhone?"

"Oh, but Caesar—" This was all too fast. "I know they'd want to say goodbye. I could call them."

No, Caesar shook his head. "Let them be with their father." His dark eye held her there a moment. "You be with their father." He lowered his head and began hoofing through the snow, his antlers wavering gently in front of her.

Bette looked at him. How lucky was Gaino, she thought. "Goodbye?"

The antlers paused a moment—that was all—then continued their gentle sway.

Bette turned and left. She followed the light through the trees, up the slope and around to the lakeside porch.

As Piorello had instructed, she landed on the sill. She did not look back. She looked inside—a golden room, glowing almost, with a fire in the wall and a pine tree standing in the middle. The family who lived there were all standing around. Most of them Bette recognized from the summer. The old woman. Her stout friend from the garden. And the children. There was the Seed Girl and her brother beside the tree, hanging its limbs with bright red balls and candles and silver moons. They looked very happy, all of them.

Bette almost didn't want to interrupt them. She wished she could stay out there in the dark, but now the old woman was rising from her place. They were all standing and starting out.

Bette called. The girl heard, and she and Piorello arrived at the sill at the same time. The girl lifted the sash and Bette hopped underneath.

It was warm inside. Piorello greeted her brightly. "This is her," he chirped, looking up at the girl. "The one I've been with."

Bette nodded. She even let the girl take her in her hand, and stroke her feathers; she'd felt her touch before. "Where are Pavel and Rhone?" she asked.

Piorello paused. He could hear something sad in her voice. "Right over there."

The girl walked them around the tree to the long shelf above the fire. There was a candle, and a long pine branch and a miniature sled there. The girl set Bette and Piorello down beside it, and with a kind word left them alone.

This sled wasn't like Caesar's. It was smoother, like stone, and so much smaller. There was only enough room inside for a dish of crushed nuts and a pair of nests. Bette hopped up and looked inside the smaller of the two. Rhone and Pavel were tucked down inside, asleep.

"They fell straight away," said Piorello softly.

"I don't blame them. They haven't slept much."

Rhone stirred at her voice. Her eyes opened dreamily. "Did you see, Mother? Isn't it beautiful?"

"Yes. It is."

Pavel lifted his head. "Is it all right—us spending the night?"

Bette turned to Piorello, who nodded. "I told them,

tonight. Then tomorrow we go out and find a place in the birches."

"The willow," said Rhone.

"Maybe the willow."

Pavel set his head back down against his sister. "You should tell Caesar to come. Caesar should see."

Bette was silent. She waited for the children to nestle down again. "Sleep," she said.

They closed their eyes.

Piorello and Bette looked down at them a moment, then quietly Piorello hopped inside the second of the nests. "It's not as nice as yours."

Bette said nothing.

"You're tired, too."

She nodded. She could hear the family in the other room, their voices bright and gay, and she knew somewhere in her heart she felt the same, but for now she climbed inside the second nest and rested her head against Piorello's wing—Piorello's wing—and tried not to feel anything at all.

PART VII

The Brows

Twenty-five

That Christmas Eve passed quietly after dinner. Elsbeth's father and brother went to bed early, they were both so tired from the journey. Miss Gulbrandsen and Mr. Doogan stayed up only slightly later, then Uncle Per took Gramma up to her room.

Elsbeth remained by the fire. She hadn't been expecting Miles and her father, so she drew them pictures for tomorrow. For her father, she drew a knight in armor. For her brother, a boy in a boat, floating on a lake filled with giant fish.

It was late when she finished. She rolled the drawings up like scrolls and tied them with ribbon, then set them down among all the rest of the presents, which cluttered around the base of the tree like the rubble of a fallen gift-tower.

She thought she must be the last awake in the house, so next she damped the tree candles, all but one, which she kept for herself. She took one last peek at the birds, sound asleep in their nests, then made her way out to the front hall.

She was at the first stair and heading up when she heard someone whisper her name. "Elsbeth."

It was Miss Gulbrandsen, standing over at the door of the dining room. She was in her robe. "Did you forget?"

"What?"

Miss Gulbrandsen gave a nod in the direction of the library. "It's Christmas Eve."

She nodded again, this time back toward the kitchen.

"Oh." Elsbeth descended the stair and followed.

The ingredients were all out on the counter—the cereal, the bowl, and a spoon. Miss Gulbrandsen had already set some water on the flame. It was boiling now. She let Elsbeth drop in four scoops of oatmeal, and they waited quietly.

"Late," Miss Gulbrandsen observed.

Elsbeth yawned.

Soon the porridge was thick and steaming. Miss Gulbrandsen spooned it into the bowl.

"Butter?"

Miss Gulbrandsen gave a firm nod. Elsbeth cut a wedge from the dish and lopped it on.

"Sugar?"

"Brown." Miss Gulbrandsen pointed to the jar, and Elsbeth dusted a spoonful over the top.

"Cream?"

Again, Miss Gulbrandsen nodded. As Elsbeth went to fill the creamer, Miss Gulbrandsen poured a glass of water. They set everything on her grandmother's tray, with a linen and a spoon, then started back for the library together, candles out front.

. . .

The house lights had dimmed one by one while Caesar finished off the moss beneath the snow. Now the moss was gone, and the house was dark, all but for the tiny flames which flickered just behind every window.

He had to go now, start back for Gaino. But the antlers weighed heavily on Caesar's neck, and the flickering lights all seemed to beckon him: To see the children one more time. To give them something as well.

Head low, he stepped out from behind the short pines and started up the slope, on quiet, even steps.

There was only one window he could reach, right

215

at the corner of the house. It was slimmer than the others, and slanted to face the woods. Caesar walked directly up and looked inside.

There was a candle here, too. He could only barely see the room behind, it was so dark. He turned his one good eye and looked for some sign of the birds, but the only shapes he could make out were over in the far corner—a strange cluster of shadows. They didn't make sense. There was the head and antlers of another reindeer—just the head and antlers, floating against the wall. Beside it was a much larger figure. It looked like a bear almost, standing with its arms outstretched, but it was too still—not like a bear at all. Last was an owl, and of the three, the owl was the only one who really seemed to be there. He was perched on a post beside the other two, and staring right back at Caesar.

But just then two lights flickered into view over by the door, and hovered there a moment, like a pair of fireflies.

. . .

"Tibel?" whispered Elsbeth. "We brought you something."

Both Elsbeth and Miss Gulbrandsen waited for an answer, but the room was silent.

Elsbeth entered gingerly. She walked straight up to the hearth, knelt down at the flagstone, and unloaded the tray—first the linen mat, then the spoon, the creamer, the glass of water, and finally the bowl of porridge.

She stood. "Tibel?"

No answer.

"Merry Christmas."

The room was still.

"Come." Miss Gulbrandsen waved her back to the door. "Let him be."

Elsbeth took her candle and tiptoed back out, without once looking at either the owl or the corner window.

. . .

Caesar did not stay long. As soon as the girl was gone, he looked back up at the owl. It did not call, or even move, but its eyes told Caesar not to worry. The sparrows were here, safe inside. He could go.

Caesar turned from the window and descended the slope again. He followed his tracks back into the woods, through the birches all the way to the willow.

There he stopped. The house was just barely visible through the branches. Caesar bowed his head before the bath. He hooked his antlers around the stone pedestal and began twisting his neck back and forth, back and forth. The only sound in all the wood was the scuffing of Caesar's antlers against the stone, and the low murmur of his breath. Back and forth he turned his head, then with a sudden jerk, the left antler fell to the snow. For the first time he saw the splintered brow. He kept his head low and gave another twist. The second antler fell. For the first time he saw the nest, fastened to its tine, and swaddled in his velvet.

Caesar raised his head, his crown now bare, and rounded to the lakeside of the tree. One last time he looked back at the house. It stood, calm and warm, whispering smoke into the sky. Caesar took a length of willow in his mouth, then turned and started back across the frozen lake, for Gaino.